Teen Superheroes Book Four:

The Twisted Future

Find out more about Darrell at his website:

http://www.darrellpitt.com

Email: darrellpitt@gmail.com

Dedicated

To Richard Matheson

Prolog

My name is Axel.

I'm one of a group of teenagers who had their memories wiped and were given incredible powers. I can control air, turn it into cannonballs, create invisible shields or use it so I can fly at amazing speeds. I'm American, but don't ask me what state I'm from because I don't know.

The next member of our team is Brodie, a red-headed Australian with the strength and speed of three grown men. She's also my girlfriend which means I think she's sweet and lovable—even though she can take my head off with one punch.

Then there's Chad. He's Norwegian, blond, brave and—well, a complete egotistical idiot—but still a friend. He can create and manipulate fire and ice. His sister is Ebony, the quiet member of the team. She can transmute elements so if you have a rose she can turn it to gold or silver or carbon. It's a cool power to have.

The youngest member of our team is Dan, a

boy from China. He can control metal with his mind, but he can also control other people's minds or read their thoughts. Sometimes. It's not a very reliable power so he doesn't use it much.

Last, but not least, there's Ferdy. He's brilliant, but he's also autistic. Sometimes he's hard to communicate with, but that doesn't mean he's any less a person than any of us. You mess with him, you mess with all of us.

We were given our powers by the Agency who were a secret organization in cahoots with aliens known as the Bakari. I say *were* because an alien spacecraft recently crashed to Earth with the peoples of a hundred planets on board. Everyone now knows about the Agency and the Bakari. Not only do they know there's life on other planets, the refugees of that ship are now living in a makeshift town called New Haven, located in Virginia. People aren't allowed to visit and the aliens aren't allowed to leave. The whole situation is still being worked out by the United Nations.

Everything changed for us during our last

adventure. I had a little misunderstanding with the Russian government which meant I ended up being labeled a criminal. Ferdy lost his life while saving the planet—but then he got it back again. His body was destroyed by a device called the Solar Accelerator, but his consciousness was transferred to an alien warship we've christened the *Liber8tor*.

I got put into jail for my actions, but then my friends broke me out and now we're on the run from the Agency, and every government on the planet.

Yeah, I know it all sounds weird, but weird is our business.

At least things can't get any worse.

Can they?

Chapter One

'Three flex craft are approaching at Mach Four,' Ferdy said.

'How far away?' I asked.

'1000 miles and closing.'

We were sitting on the bridge of the *Liber8tor*. The name had been decided upon by the others while I was still in jail. *Liber8tor* had been owned by a race known as the Tagaar. It had eight decks of accommodation, torpedoes, laser weapons and a cloaking device. The interior was a cross between the inside of a submarine and the skin of a green lizard. Whoever did the Tagaar's interior decorating needed talking to.

The others had a basic understanding of how the vessel worked, but it was still a complete mystery to me. As was Ferdy and his relationship to the ship. His consciousness was contained inside the *Liter8tor* computer. He was alive, but trapped. I could not even imagine what that would be like. At least it was better than the alternative.

Each of our stations—navigation, weapons, science, environmental and engineering—surrounded the helm. The huge view screen before us showed little, just a vast expanse of ocean and sky. We had hoped we might be lucky, evading capture by flying loops over the Pacific.

It seemed luck was not on our side.

Dan, despite being the youngest of our group, was helmsman. We'd all taken turns flying the ship, but Dan seemed to have a natural affinity with the controls. Maybe all those computer games were finally paying off.

The others knew their assigned roles. Ebony was navigation, Chad weapons and Brodie science. I was in charge of environmental systems, which meant I was clueless, as I was still trying to learn the Tagaar language.

Pushing back his black hair, Dan leant forward in his seat and gripped the controls. We felt a slight acceleration as he increased engine thrust.

'Are you sure you know what you're doing?' Chad asked.

'No,' Dan said. 'I've completely forgotten how to fly this ship and we're all about to die.'

'That's really funny,' Chad said, flashing a look at me. 'Don't you hate smart kids?'

'Yeah,' I said. 'But I've grown fond of you anyway.'

'Hardy-har-har.'

'The flex craft are continuing to close on our position.' Ferdy's voice was clear and without panic. 'The first Prime Minister of Australia was Edmund Barton.'

'That's handy to know,' Brodie said.

'Funny,' Ebony said, smiling. 'I was just about to ask you that. Can you read minds, Ferdy?'

'Is Ebony making a joke?' Ferdy asked.

'Ebony is making—I mean—yes, I am.'

'Then it is a funny joke.'

'How are those Flex craft?' Brodie's face was calm, but her fists were tightly clenched. 'Are we losing them?'

Brodie didn't like to be at the mercy of events. I sometimes joked she wasn't happy unless she was

7

hitting someone. Or maybe I wasn't joking.

'Quite the opposite,' Ferdy said. 'The ships are closing with three more vessels converging from the west.'

I swallowed hard. The Agency had declared us international criminals and had been pursuing us relentlessly for weeks. Every time we thought we were safe, they turned up again. *Liber8tor* had a cloaking device, but they seemed able to see through it like glass.

'That's six ships,' Chad said.

'You can count?' Dan looked impressed as he tapped controls on his panel and the engines gave another surge of acceleration. 'Ferdy? Can those flex craft follow into orbit?'

'It is impossible to know if their systems have been modified for spaceflight.'

'Hmm.'

I wasn't sure what that meant. 'Does that mean we're going into orbit?' I asked. 'Or will we just try to outrun them?'

'Hmm.'

'Or are we about to die?'

'Hmm.'

Now I felt as worried as Chad looked.

'What exactly does "hmm" mean?' Brodie asked.

'It means we're going to do the unexpected.' The scene in the view screen shifted as *Liber8tor* angled towards the Pacific Ocean. 'We're going down.'

'Is Dan about to test the new modifications?' Ferdy asked.

'Now's as good a time as any.'

Chad acted like he'd been stung. 'Modifications? What modifications?' he asked. 'Why don't I know anything about this?'

'They're on the notice board,' Dan said.

'What notice board?'

'On level nine.'

'Level nine? Where the hell's level nine?'

'Just above level eight.'

I would have laughed if I weren't so worried. There was no level nine.

The ship's speed increased and Chad fell to silence as we accelerated towards the ocean. White waves and spray appeared. Then, at seemingly the last instant, Dan adjusted our angle of descent so we skimmed low over the waves.

'Flex craft are closing on all sides,' Ferdy reported. 'The closest is one thousand feet...five hundred...'

'Hang onto your hats,' Dan said.

I looked at Ebony. Swallowing, she gripped the arm rests of her seat. She appeared small and vulnerable, so I gave her a comforting smile. Then I glanced at Brodie, who just glared at me.

'What?' I said.

How could someone be jealous at a time like this?

The *Liber8tor* hitting the ocean felt like we'd slammed into concrete. A vast spray of water obliterated the screen, followed by a wash of bubbles. We saw shimmering blue-green water cut by bands of sunlight. A school of startled fish zoomed away.

'We're underwater!' I said.

'Really?' Chad's voice had gone up a notch. 'I hadn't noticed!'

'The *Liber8tor* is at five hundred feet and descending,' Ferdy said. 'And the second highest mountain in the world is K2.'

'Thanks for letting me know,' Chad said, looking green.

'You're most welcome, friend Chad.'

'No, I wasn't—I mean, never mind...' He stopped. 'Are we safe down here?'

'That is impossible to say,' Ferdy said. 'Although Ferdy can calculate many possible futures, often with great accuracy.'

This was news to me.

'You're saying you can see the future?' I asked.

'Ferdy is simply able to calculate the possibilities of many different courses of action.'

'So are those Flex fighters going to follow us?' I asked.

'It is unlikely their craft have been modified to travel underwater,' Ferdy said, 'which is fortunate because *Liber8tor*'s chances of surviving an air battle with six flex craft was no better than one chance in eighty-two.'

'Lucky for us,' I said. 'Unlucky for them.'

Chapter Two

'Mr. Price?'

'Yes?'

Agent Palmer peered at the gaunt young man sitting in the waiting room. He had an untidy mop of black hair, unwashed clothing and looked like someone who rarely left his basement. *Another recluse living on corn chips and cola,* she sighed. Palmer had dealt with all sorts of people since being put in charge of New Projects, the latest initiative by the Agency. Some of the people had been quite brilliant. A few had been crackpots. One or two had required a call to security, and a straitjacket.

'I'm sorry to have kept you waiting,' she said.

'I've waited weeks for this appointment.'

'I'm sorry,' she repeated. 'We've had a backlog since the Agency went public.'

Give me the good old days, Palmer thought. *It was a simpler time, but—*

'Agent Palmer?' The young man scowled. 'If you don't mind...'

The agent led Price down a wide corridor clad in glass and steel. The building, located in Lower Manhattan, employed more than a thousand people, with more joining every day. Everyone wanted a role in this new world. Palmer surreptitiously glanced at her watch. *Price better not be another crackpot.* She was only twenty minutes away from lunch.

They entered her office where her receptionist, Carl Jackson, sat at his computer. He was an army private, a tall black man with a stutter and a sixty word per minute typing speed. Offering Price a seat, Palmer noticed he was carrying an old doctor's bag.

What's in there?

She glanced down at the file of information Jackson had gleaned about Price. There wasn't a lot, but it was interesting. James Price was older than he looked, twenty-two, and had completed a double major in chemistry and physics at UCLA, his specialty being rare elements.

'Today we're going to change history,' Price began.

'Really. How?'

James Price seemed not to hear her. 'I've been working on my device for almost ten years.'

'Ten years...' Palmer did the calculations. 'So you started—'

'When I was twelve.'

She nodded. 'And what does it do?'

'It's a TDR. A trans-dimensional resonator.'

'And...'

'It siphons energy from an alternate dimension,' he explained, 'providing free and perpetual energy—forever.'

It took Agent Palmer a moment to put it all together. 'It collects energy from another dimension?' she said.

'That's right,' he said. 'Endless amounts of it.'

He pulled something from the bag that looked like a cross between an old sewing machine and a gramophone. Most of the parts were hand crafted from brass or steel with wires running from a control panel to a cone resembling an early twentieth-century loud speaker.

Inwardly groaning, Agent Palmer peeked at

the clock on her desk.

Lunch in ten minutes, she thought. *What will it be today? They make a good pasta at*—

A whirring came from James Price's machine as a thin slither of light projected from its conical end.

'What is that?' Palmer asked, peering at the light. 'Exactly?'

'It's the future.' Price sounded breathless as if he had been running a marathon. 'Perpetual energy.'

'It's...it's...' Palmer was lost for words. 'It's very little. And bright.'

Price laughed, looking geekier than ever. 'But very powerful,' he said. 'It runs on Francium.'

'Francium. What's that?'

'Francium is one of the world's rarest elements.'

'And it's taken you ten years—'

'Francium isn't easy to come by, but my device—the trans-dimensional resonator—uses it to crack open a hole in the dimensional fabric of—'

'Hold on.' Agent Palmer held up a hand. 'Explain this to me like I'm a dummy.'

'You are a dummy,' Price said, as if it were obvious. 'Most people are. That's why a TDR has never been invented before.'

'TDR?'

'I told you before. The trans-dimensional resonator.'

'Explain it to me. Slowly.'

'Okay, you're familiar with the big bang—'

Fortunately, James Price was able to condense the entire history of the universe into a few short lines of explanation. 'The big bang created multiple dimensions,' he explained. 'A infinite number of universes. Every single action since then has resulted in the birth of new universes, with an infinite number being created every second.'

'I'm familiar with that idea.' It was often bandied about in science fiction stories. Alternate realities where John F Kennedy had not been assassinated, dinosaurs still roamed the Earth and where the South won the American Civil War. 'What's that got to do with your invention?'

'One of those many realities is where the big

bang occurred and is still a mass of hot, subatomic particles. It was, after all, chance that led to the formation of galaxies, solar systems and planets.'

Palmer nodded as if she understood. 'Of course.'

'The TDR simply opens a crack into one of those dimensions and siphons off energy. That's what we're seeing right now. Energy flowing from that crack.'

'You've cracked open the universe, and the light coming from your...gramophone is from a different reality.'

'Right.'

'That's...' Palmer struggled for words. 'Crazy. It's the most insane thing I've ever heard.'

Price's face darkened. 'Great minds have always fought to be recognized by lesser beings.'

'That's always a problem, I'm sure.' Agent Palmer eyed the computer. *Lunchtime!* 'Thanks for coming in to see us—'

'I have harnessed the power of the universe!' Price said, furious. He punched a switch on his device. 'And you will recognize that power!'

The tiny spear of light expanded into a bright orange globe the size of a chair. It flew upwards, punching a hole in the ceiling. Palmer yelled and fell backwards onto the floor. Private Jackson raced in, but skidded to a halt in astonishment.

Agent Palmer rounded her desk as James Price snapped off his machine. She peered up into the gap as people from all eighty-eight floors stared back down. Beyond them she caught a glimpse of blue sky.

'Sit down, Mr. Price,' Agent Palmer said. 'And tell me again how this device works—starting with the Big Bang.'

Chapter Three

An hour had passed since we'd descended into the depths of the ocean and we were in *Liber8tor*'s galley.

Dan had the ship on autopilot which allowed him to join us while we cut through the water. The Agency ships had given up—for now.

I inserted five plastic bags of green goo into the Tagaar equivalent of a microwave, pushed a button and waited a few seconds. The oven beeped. I removed the bags and passed them around. Chad opened his and sniffed cautiously at the contents.

'Is this another packet of—'

'K'tresh?'

Ferdy had found the name in the Tagaar database. Not only was it hard to describe K'tresh, it was even harder to eat. The taste was a mixture of fish and avocado, but with the consistency of grease. Ferdy had assured us it was highly nutritious and completely safe for human consumption.

Still, it wouldn't have surprised me if

someone started growing a second head.

Ebony peered at the plate. 'There's only one thing wrong with this.'

'That is?'

'The taste. Oh, and the look...and the smell...and...'

'I get the idea.'

Brodie spoke up. 'We need some fresh food. And a holiday.'

She was right about that. While we weren't at the top of the FBI's most wanted list, we were on it, sandwiched between serial killers, armed robbers and terrorists. It wasn't a good list to be on. The stress wasn't easy to take.

'There is an island approximately thirty nautical miles from our current position,' Ferdy's voice came over the loud speaker. 'Rousseau island.'

'Whassat?' Chad said.

Ferdy spelt the word. 'Named after the French explorer who first discovered it in 1863, it was briefly occupied by a colony before being eventually abandoned.'

'Why did they leave?' I asked.

'They deemed it to have no commercial value, and it is far off the shipping lanes.'

'So no-one lives there?' I said. 'That could prove the ideal place for us to settle down.'

'That's right,' Chad said. 'Plant lawns. Raise a few kids. Drink beer on the porch while watching TV—'

'I know what you mean,' Brodie said, ignoring Chad. 'Maybe we could set up a base of operations.'

'And there would be fresh food,' Ebony added.

'Fresh food,' Chad echoed, warming to the idea. 'No more K'tresh.'

'Oh, I don't know,' I said. 'K'tresh sort of grows on you after a while.'

'Yeah. Like mold.'

I liked the idea of an island base. *Liber8tor* was a good ship, but built for a race of warriors, not for comfort. The ship was even capable of interplanetary flight, but that wasn't on the agenda.

Not yet.

Returning to the bridge, I sat down at the environmental console while the others checked their controls. I could only make out a few words in Tagaar. As far as I could tell, *Liber8tor* was fully operational. Or I hoped it was, anyway.

The clear waters of the Pacific slid past the screen.

'We are one mile from Rousseau Island,' Ferdy said.

'Have we lost the Agency pursuit ships?' Brodie asked.

'They are beyond the scope of our senses.'

'Good. Let's see this island up close.'

We broke the surface and swooped in low across a white beach. The island was a long, flat piece of land covered in palm trees and thick foliage with a lake in the middle, and a small mountain at the Northern end. A flock of white birds take off in alarm as we approached.

'Looks like it's time for chicks and guys to do what comes naturally,' Chad said, grinning.

'Uh, what's that?' Brodie asked.

'You know...get down with nature...walk naked among the trees...'

'You should do that.'

'Uh...' Chad went pink as a ghost of a smile creased Brodie's lips. Months ago, she would have rolled her eyes. Now she was teasing him. This was something new. Something had changed between them while I was in jail.

Or had anything *happened* between them?

No-one had said anything, but maybe they wouldn't if Brodie had cheated on me. They may have decided to keep it secret rather than hurt my feelings. I tried pushing the thought from my mind. It was ridiculous. Brodie was my girlfriend. Chad was my friend, maybe my best friend, considering everything we'd been through.

Dan brought the ship down into a small clearing a hundred feet from the beach. We made our way down three levels and stepped out into warm sunshine and fresh air. It was like landing on another world after weeks inside the Tagaar ship.

'I'd forgotten what the outside world smelt like,' Ebony said. 'I am so sick of that ship.' She added, 'No offense, Ferdy.'

We all wore wrist communicators that allowed us to speak to each other. They even had a video screen so you could see the caller if you wanted.

'No offense is taken, friend Ebony,' Ferdy said. 'The eighth element on the periodic table is oxygen.'

'Is it?' Ebony said. 'That's great.'

Brodie's eyes swept the jungle. 'How fantastic to not be on the run anymore,' she said. 'To be free of the Agency.'

'You didn't have to be a criminal,' I pointed out. 'You could have left me in jail.'

'No, we couldn't.' She drew close and kissed my cheek. 'Where you go, we all go.'

I watched a seagull arc towards the ocean. My month in jail wasn't fun. I had expected to spend decades behind bars for kidnapping the Russian Premier. Instead, here I was a few weeks later on an island in the Pacific, the sun on my face and my girlfriend at my side.

'Let's explore,' Dan suggested.

'Is it safe?' Ebony said.

'What can possibly go wrong?' Chad asked.

I peered through the jungle curtain, making out three distinct layers of foliage. Traipsing through that wouldn't be easy. Visibility was only a few feet. Having superpowers meant we could handle most situations, but it didn't make us indestructible. A wild animal could kill us as easily as anyone else.

'What's that?' Dan asked.

We turned to see him staring at the sky. A tiny black cut had appeared in the clear blue expanse. For a second I thought it might have been an aircraft, but then it grew larger as a low pulse filled the air.

'Beats me,' Brodie said. 'But I think something's inside it.'

The cut in the sky grew larger until it was as large as the clearing. Within it was a distant glint of silver. A spaceship.

I tapped the communicator on my wrist. 'Ferdy, what are we looking at?'

'A temporal distortion has formed above us,' Ferdy said calmly. 'Within it is a vessel.'

'Ferdy,' Chad groaned. 'What does that mean?'

'Ferdy is not sure he can explain. Suffice to say, a hole has formed in the time/space continuum and a vessel is entering our universe.'

'Let's get back into the ship,' Ebony suggested. 'It would be safer—'

The alien vessel suddenly grew larger and flew from the gap. The black cut disappeared as the ship zoomed low over the jungle. Without a sound, the ship completed a slow turn around the mountain before heading towards us. Decelerating as braking thrusters fired, it landed next to *Liber8tor*.

No-one spoke. We were so amazed by this sudden turn of events that we couldn't think of anything to say. Now I stared more closely at the vessel and realized that, although it had wings and rear thrusters that enabled flight, there were no visible windows. A squat ship, it was as if someone had taken a jumbo jet, cut out the middle and stuck both ends together. The vessel's tiny wings were too small to actually fly it, but somehow they worked.

Sheets of ice broke away as a hatch cracked open, slowly swinging upwards. The interior was dark, but then a man stepped out.

Brodie turned to me. 'That man,' she gasped. 'He looks...'

I stared at him in amazement. He was tall and thin with brown hair and eyes. Millions of people fitted that description, but there was no mistaking the similarity. Chad also did a double-take. 'He looks like you,' he said.

'I'm sorry to take you all by surprise,' the man said in a familiar voice.

I knew that voice!

He continued. 'It's a miracle I'm here at all.'

'Are we related?' I asked. 'We look the same.'

'We *are* the same,' the man said. 'I'm you—from forty years in the future.'

Chapter Four

It wasn't often that we were struck dumb, but this was one of those times. We stared in amazement at the stranger.

'Did you hear me?' he asked. 'I said that I'm you from the future. I'm here because we need to change history and you're the only people who can do it.'

'You're...me.' I struggled to come to terms with what he was saying. This old guy was me. The future version of me. 'You've come from the future...and...'

He shook his head in annoyance. 'I don't remember ever being this dense,' he said. 'It's a lot to take it, but I need you to all wake up and listen to me.'

'We're awake,' Chad said, 'but it doesn't mean we're about to start changing our plans for the day.'

'You haven't changed a bit, Chad. Still the same pain in the—'

'How do I know you're me?' I interrupted. 'That you're not a...robot or something?'

'Those are good questions,' the man said. 'Why don't we ask Ferdy?'

That he even knew about Ferdy was a point in his favor, but it wasn't enough to convince me.

'Ferdy,' Ebony said. 'Who is this guy? Is he really Axel? From the future?'

Ferdy's voice came over the communicators. 'It is impossible to ascertain whether this individual is actually Axel. A DNA test would confirm his identity, but Ferdy *can* confirm his vessel is capable of time travel.'

'Couldn't this guy just be an alien?' Brodie asked. 'An imposter?'

'The *Liber8tor*'s sensors indicate he is human.'

'But he could be a clone. Couldn't he? Even with a DNA test.'

'That is true.'

'Prove it.' This time it was Dan who spoke. 'Tell us something that only Axel would know.'

'Something not embarrassing,' I said. 'I don't want to look stupid.'

'I have no desire to make myself look foolish. Either my younger or older self.' The man thought for a long moment. 'All right. You were in jail a few weeks ago for the kidnapping of the Russian Premier. You wrote in your diary every single day.'

'That doesn't mean anything,' I said. 'Anyone from the jail might know that.'

'Fine. How about this? You were captured by Typhoid after first acquiring your powers. A psycho by the name of Doctor Ravana tortured you for information. You thought you were going to die, but Brodie helped you escape.'

That was true. Horrible, but true.

'That's no secret,' Dan said. 'A lot of people could know that.'

'Not really,' Ebony said, frowning. 'People in the Agency would know. People within Typhoid.' She stared at the stranger. 'But just not anyone.'

'We went to the roof,' the man continued, his eyes locked on mine. 'I wouldn't jump between the

31

buildings. But I eventually did.'

It all seemed a long time ago now, but it had only been a few months. I was captured by Typhoid. Brodie helped me escape. We went to the roof. I eventually jumped, but I ended up falling through a window on the top floor of the building opposite. Then—

'You were attacked by an old lady with a broom,' the man said. 'And you've never told anyone. No-one has known. Not until now.'

I thought hard. He was right. The memory had almost faded from my mind. The old lady living in the apartment had hit me with a broom after I demolished her window. It was a minor detail, something so unimportant I had never shared it with anyone. How could he know? *How could he know unless he was me?*

He spent the next five minutes sharing other memories, other events I had not told the others. The time I was ill from Ebony's cooking, but had not informed anyone because I didn't want to offend her. Another time I had gone out looking at the stars and fallen into a ditch. By the time he finished talking I found myself staring at him open-mouthed.

'Does that sound right?' Chad asked me. 'Is it all true?'

'It's true,' I said, nodding. 'I don't recall ever telling anyone that stuff.'

'Good.' Old Axel looked satisfied. 'So now we can move on.'

'Move onto what?' Brodie asked.

'I need your help.'

'You've already said that, but I don't know why. You're the one with the time machine, and all.'

'A time machine doesn't make you God,' he said. 'I'll tell you what I can, but I can't tell you about your futures. It would contaminate the time line, causing irreparable damage to the space/time continuum.'

'Sounds messy,' Chad sighed. 'We wouldn't want to do that. Would we?'

Old Axel's eyes narrowed. *He doesn't like Chad*, I thought. No. It was more than that. He *hated* Chad.

My older self continued. 'The world is a different place in forty years. It's—'

'It's like Disneyland?' Chad suggested.

'—it's like your worst nightmare,' Old Axel said. 'The atmosphere is failing. The natural resources are gone. Humanity is facing extinction.'

Chapter Five

'Extinction?' Ebony repeated the word, ashen-faced.

'I can't tell you the details,' Old Axel continued, 'but I can tell you this: the man responsible is James Price.'

'Who's he?' I asked.

'In this era, a scientist. In the future, a dictator. A monster. He has to be stopped.'

Brodie frowned. 'And how do we stop him?'

'He has to be killed.'

'We don't kill people,' I said, having already been down this rabbit hole. 'I once thought I could, but I felt—'

'I know.' Old Axel interrupted me. 'The Russian Premier. I was there, but this is different.'

'We're not killing anyone,' I said flatly.

Chad interrupted. 'If you're so keen to see this James Price dead, why don't you do it yourself?'

'I would if I could.'

'And why can't you?'

'This time machine is experimental. I was lucky to arrive here at this time and place.'

'So why not use your powers?' I asked.

Old Axel glared at me. 'Because I don't have any powers. I haven't had them in years.'

I was struck dumb.

'I can't say any more than that,' Old Axel said.

I felt the others looking at me. They all knew my powers had worked intermittently; sometimes they failed at the worst times. But to learn I would lose them completely...

'There's only one way to prove what you're saying is true,' Brodie said, her eyes fixed on the time machine. 'You're taking us to the future.'

'That's not possible,' Old Axel said.

'But it's happening,' Ebony said. 'Either we go to the future to confirm what you're saying or you go back by yourself.' She was a quiet girl, but sometimes she seemed to draw on some inner resolve, as if there were another person lurking inside. 'But Axel—our Axel—is right. We're not killing anyone based on a five minute conversation with a stranger.'

Old Axel looked like he wanted to argue—or just scream at us—but finally he gave a long, single nod. His eyes swept back to me. 'It's risky,' he said. 'I can't fit you all inside the machine.'

Chad turned to Dan. 'You should stay here,' he said. 'Seeing as how you're the youngest.'

Dan protested. Of course. I watched Old Axel as they argued the point. The longer I studied him, the more I felt like I was watching someone on the verge of exhaustion. Someone who had lived on the edge for too long. 'We need to get moving,' he interrupted. 'The sooner I prove this to you, the sooner we change history.'

'And I thought we had all the time in the world,' Chad said.

Old Axel did not smile. 'Dan, you're staying here,' he said. 'The rest of you into the ship. This should only take a few minutes.'

Dan looked rebellious as we boarded the time ship. He didn't appreciate being left behind. The interior was similar to an Agency flex craft, but smaller. The dashboard looked unfinished with wires and gages everywhere. A dial in the center displayed today's date and geographical coordinates.

Old Axel pulled a component, covered in blue and silver circuitry, from the console. It looked melted.

'This is the temporal resonator.' He produced another from a carry bag and slotted it into place. 'They burn out after only one journey.'

There was only one seat and he took it as we crammed behind. Pushing a button, I saw Dan give a small wave as the hatch sealed shut. It was like being locked inside a tomb.

'Say goodbye to today,' Old Axel said. 'The next stop is the future.'

Chapter Six

Dan watched as the time ship lifted off the ground. It shuddered in mid-air as a black slit appeared over the clearing. The slit increased in size until it was as big as a small house.

When the time ship had first appeared, Dan had thought the hole it passed through was black. Now he saw it looked like oil on water, with rainbows curving about the interior. Ozone filled the air. A breeze pulled at his hair as the time ship eased itself into the hole. The juncture in time and space shrank to a slit, before collapsing at both ends into a dot, and finally nothing.

The jungle closed in around Dan. It had all happened so fast he had not had time to consider the consequences of everyone leaving. Now the others were gone he felt completely alone. He was one small boy on a deserted island in the middle of the ocean.

Dan shook off the fear. He wasn't going to hide. Not when he had an island to explore. He was a modern day Robinson Crusoe, which meant his man

Friday was...

'Ferdy. Are you there?'

'Ferdy reads you loud and clear, Dan. Egypt is the world's thirtieth largest country—'

'Great. I'm going—'

'—and the most populated in the Middle East.'

'That's wonderful, Ferdy. I just wanted to let you know that I'm going explore the island.'

'That sounds exciting, Dan.'

'It should be fun.'

'Watch out for tigers.'

Dan stared into the dark jungle. 'There are tigers here?' he asked.

'Ferdy is making a joke.'

'Ha ha,' Dan forced a laugh. 'That's very funny.'

Ferdy paused. 'There is some new information that Dan should know. *Liber8tor*'s sensors are picking up possible structures near the center of the island.'

'Structures?'

'From the Latin word, *structura*, meaning—'

'That's okay, Ferdy. What direction?'

'Approximately three miles east of our current location.'

'Are there people?'

'The *Liber8tor* senses are not picking up any life forms.'

Which was Ferdy's way of saying *I don't know*. Maybe the island was completely deserted, but maybe a cannibal tribe lived here and fed on unwary travelers. He had seen a movie like that once. It was fun and games until the cannibals turned up and started eating people. Then the laughing stopped; it was hard to laugh without a face.

He peered into the jungle. Birds whistled and moved in the upper branches. A shrill shriek ended in a guttural choking sound. Undergrowth moved as something crawled across the ground. An animal raced away between distant branches.

This can't be a good idea, he thought. Why traipse off into the arms of hungry cannibals when there are completely good computer games on board

Liter8tor? Level twenty-six of *Zombie Attack Squad* was calling.

Still, buildings would mean shelter, and shelter might mean beds. Real beds. The Tagaar idea of a bed was something made from reinforced concrete. What he wouldn't give for a decent night's sleep on a real bed...

And think of how impressed the others would be when he told them what he had found. They might stop thinking of him as the kid, and decide he should now be known as Metal Man. Or Metallaton. Or Metal...something.

'I'll stay in contact,' he told Ferdy. 'Let me know if the others return.'

Dan started into the jungle. The undergrowth was dense, but the ground was level. He purposely made a racket as he pushed aside vines and palm fronds; he wanted to alert anyone—or anything—that he was coming. Hopefully snakes or lizards would bolt in the opposite direction.

Unless they were hungry, in which case...

'Relax,' he murmured. 'I may be short, but

I've got crazy superpowers. I can read minds. Sometimes. And I can control metal—'

Dan looked down. Sure, he could control metal, but he had forgotten to bring anything *made* of metal, which made his power useless.

'Good work,' he said. 'Metal-idiot-boy.'

It was dark under the canopy. The trees grew crazily as if evolution had taken a sideways step; the trunks were huge and the overhanging branches so overflowed with foliage that the ground was almost dark. Vines hung like giant spider webs. Red-and-yellow orchids lurked among ferns. Fallen trees, covered in green moss and orange fungi, cracked underfoot as Dan fought his way through the foliage.

Wiping his brow, he reached the base of a large tree. The humidity was unbelievable. *Why didn't I bring a drink?* Then he noticed a small stream under some nearby palms. He thirstily drank a mouthful. *Refreshing.*

Continuing up a hill, he was beginning to wonder if these buildings were just a figment of Ferdy's computer imagination, when he spotted a gray shape among the foliage. He brushed aside some palms. A ten-foot concrete wall, smattered in moss, ran in both directions. He stepped back. Whoever had built this thing was serious about keeping people out. Picking a direction at random, he followed it to a clearing and found the remains of an old road, hopelessly overgrown, leading to pair of rusted metal gates.

What was this place?

The gates were locked, but the chain was rusty and easily snapped when Dan applied his powers to it. He squeezed through and found an overgrown enclosure. An old jeep rusted in a corner; a fully grown palm tree grew from the back seat. A long, low building nestled under trees. Vines grew through the half-a-dozen broken windows running across the front.

Dan tried a door. Locked. Focusing on it, he snapped it open. The interior was a large, square room with a closed door on the other side. A broken light bulb hung from the ceiling. The place smelt like compost.

'Do I really want to do this?' he murmured.

It would be much easier to return to the ship. Back there waited *Zombie Attack Squad* and comfort, of a kind. But that would be running away, and Axel, Chad and the others wouldn't hesitate to enter. They would just march straight in.

He sighed. If they could do it, so could he.

He strode across the room. He was about half-way across when the floor cracked beneath him. It shuddered, gave a mighty groan and collapsed.

Chapter Seven

'Hold on,' Old Axel warned. 'This could get bumpy.'

He wasn't kidding. No sooner had we entered the black rift than the ship tilted crazily. Crying out, we all crashed to one side. Ebony fell onto me and I held her tightly for a few seconds until the ship leveled out.

'Are you okay?' Brodie asked, frowning at me holding Ebony. 'I wouldn't want you to get hurt.'

'I'm fine,' I said. 'It isn't as if—'

'Cut the chatter!' Old Axel snapped.

He was a real barrel of fun. We were falling down a corridor filled with long pools of black oil, each ringed by a rainbow loop. The time ship itself was virtually silent, the only sound a gentle hum from the engines.

'Shame they don't put in more seats,' Chad said.

'This ship is a prototype,' Old Axel explained. 'The Agency lost half-a-dozen before they worked properly.'

'Lost?' I asked. 'Where?'

'Who knows? Some of them started by themselves and disappeared into infinity.'

Disappeared into infinity? I hoped they'd ironed out all the bugs. If something broke, we might end up fighting dinosaurs in the distant past. Or trying to survive in the far future when the sun has burnt out.

'How long will this take?' Brodie asked.

'Only a few minutes, but there's a couple of things we've got to cover before we land.'

'Like what?'

'The skies are a no fly zone, but we'll be arriving over the badlands. They don't monitor the badlands.'

'The badlands?' I said. 'That sounds...bad.'

'It will give you a chance to see what the future is like. You'll see why it's important that James Price be stopped. Permanently.'

The vessel jolted again. Ebony glanced at me, giving me a nervous smile. I liked Ebony. Not like I liked Brodie. I was in love with Brodie. I just wished she weren't so jealous. I saw Chad give Brodie a sideway's glance and my stomach gave a small lurch—not brought on by the movement of the ship. Chad was a friend. One of my best friends, despite being a huge pain in the anatomy. He was probably attracted to Brodie, but he was attracted to just about every girl we encountered.

'We're leaving the rift,' Old Axel said. 'Hold on tight.'

Unfortunately there was nothing to hold onto, but we braced ourselves against the bulkhead as the ship headed towards a thin line of blue. It grew larger until it filled the entire screen.

Then we were through.

A city lay beneath us—or what remained of it. It looked like a war zone. Skyscrapers were broken, derelict and decaying, with not a single intact window. A lot of buildings had been destroyed by fire. Others were reduced to rubble.

The streets were choked with corroded motor vehicles; chaotic traffic jams, decades old, blocked most streets. Weeds grew through the footpaths and roads. Small fires burnt from a dozen places.

I caught sight of what was once a harbor. The water had turned into soupy white sand. The sky was blue, but unnaturally pale as if bleached. I thought I had never seen anything like this before, but then I knew I had. I knew this place. This was New York— the island of Manhattan. In the distance stood the Statue of Liberty, or what remained of her. The grand old lady had lost her head and both arms. A huge wall enveloped the entire area. Beyond lay a hazy brown mist.

Old Axel cursed. 'We're over the city!' he yelled. 'I must have gotten the coordinates wrong.'

An object arced over the skyline towards us.

'A missile!' Chad yelled. 'Watch—'

Old Axel yanked the flight stick to one side and we slammed into the bulkhead. Brodie sagged, unconscious as the time ship spun completely out of control. One second I was on the wall; the next I was against the ceiling.

Old Axel fought with the controls. 'I'm taking us down!' he screamed. 'We won't last a minute up here!'

A building filled the window; I thought we were about to die. At the last possible instant, Old Axel pulled the ship to starboard and we narrowly missed it. I was supposed to be some kind of super-powered human and yet I felt like a ball in a pinball machine. A narrow street, scattered with debris, appeared from nowhere. The vessel drew level with it, bounced twice and slid along the road.

'Everyone out!' Old Axel yelled.

This was all happening so fast. We were a tangle of arms and legs on the floor. Chad's armpit was in my face. Ebony's foot was jammed in my groin. Old Axel climbed over us and shoved open the hatch. I fell out after him.

'Hey!' Chad yelled.

He was struggling out the door with an unconscious Brodie in his arms. A whine came from down the street. Something flashed down the narrow corridor of demolished buildings towards us.

A missile.

I flung out a hand and created a shield—just in

time. The missile exploded, raining debris and shrapnel around us. Another missile curved down an alley. Ebony created a metal spear from the air and arrowed it at the weapon. It exploded before it could reach us.

'We've got to get out of here!' Ebony yelled.

A bright red ball fell from the sky and plummeted into the ground. A shapeless lump of goo. Then it shimmered and expanded into a bright red statue of a man.

'You've violated Agency airspace!' he snarled. 'Surrender yourself!'

'Talk to my lawyer!' I snapped. We had only been in the future a few minutes and already everyone wanted us dead. If he was looking for a fight then I was happy to comply.

He flung an arm out and the appendage stretched down an alley, around a tottering brownstone and back to him. It was like he was made from rubber. He pulled tight. The building groaned as he pulled it off its foundations—and straight onto us.

Chapter Eight

I threw up a barrier and the building slammed into it, burying us under tons of brick, glass and timber. One more second and we would have been dead. I focused hard, expanded the shield and pushed the debris away. Sky appeared and we scrambled free. Chad still had Brodie, unconscious, in his arms.

'Get her out of here!' I yelled.

Ebony shoved me aside and I swung around to see the red man draw back his fist. He fired it at me, but Ebony had already constructed a metal shield. His fist slammed into it and I heard a resounding cry.

Good, I thought. *I hope that hurt.*

I pushed Ebony's shield forward and used it like a battering ram, slamming it into the red man. He flew backwards into a building. I shot Ebony a smile.

'Thanks,' I said. 'I need all the help I can get.'

The red man scrambled from the front window of the building. 'Unauthorized mods are punishable by death!' he said.

'And I thought we were in real trouble!'

I fired a series of air balls at him, and he buckled under the attack. At the same time, Ebony touched the ground and turned the road under him into air. He fell twenty feet to the bottom. I peered back to check on Chad and Brodie, but they were gone. The only person visible was Old Axel.

'Come on!' he yelled.

I'd forgotten all about him in the chaos. Ebony cried out and I turned to see the red man leap straight from the hole into the sky. We stumbled over debris to an alley on the opposite side of the street. Looking back, I looked for Chad and Brodie, but still couldn't see them.

'They went the other way,' Old Axel said. 'They're safe.'

I wasn't sure I agreed with his definition of safe, but this was no time to debate it. The red man would be back in seconds. I glanced up. He was spinning back towards Earth—straight towards us. The fastest way out of here was flying, but taking to the skies was asking for trouble, so I fired another series of air cannonballs at him.

They hit, driving him sideways into a building, but he bounced straight out again, landing in front of me. He punched me in the stomach. The blow would have killed anyone else, but at the last moment I erected a shield around my body. Still, the impact threw me to the ground.

Ebony pointed at the air above the red man. A huge metal ball appeared. He had just enough time to see it before gravity took over. The ball slammed into him, pushing him into the ground. He disappeared from sight.

'Did I kill him?' Ebony asked.

'I'm not sure.' If he wasn't dead, then he was probably badly injured. I hated the idea of hurting anyone, but I didn't have a choice.

Old Axel grabbed my arm. 'Follow me.'

He dragged us towards an old department store. The front was boarded up, but he eased open a paling and pushed us through. I peered into the gloom and saw dusty shop fittings and mannequins. Then one of the mannequins moved.

'You can't come in here.' It was an old man,

unshaven and rough looking. 'You can't come in—'

'Shut up,' Old Axel snapped. 'Is there another way out?'

'A way out?' His eyes darted about in confusion. 'Have you seen my wife? She left to buy flowers.'

He continued to rave uncontrollably. I felt sorry for him. He had obviously been driven mad.

'We're friends,' Ebony said gently. 'Is there a back exit?'

'Quiet!' Old Axel hissed. 'They're here.'

Ebony and I hurried to the front. Peering through a gap in the palings, we saw half-a-dozen armed men charging down the street with guns raised. I heard the old man behind us start to speak. Old Axel cut him off. The armed guards wore uniforms that were oddly familiar, similar to those worn by security guards at the Agency, but more militarized with epaulets and insignia.

They grouped around the hole in the street. Something moved near their feet. Something red.

The hand of the red man. He struggled onto

the footpath. Obviously he was in no state to pursue us. The guards spoke to him for a moment before he nodded, gathered himself up and leapt into the sky.

The guards turned away; they were giving up. We breathed a sigh of relief as they disappeared.

'They're gone,' I said quietly. 'We should see if—'

Ebony's turned and her face fell in horror. 'No!' she cried. 'What have you done?'

Old Axel stood over the body of the old man. The stranger lay on the ground, his eyes open and staring. His neck had been broken.

Chapter Nine

'I did what I had to do,' Old Axel said. 'He was trying to speak—'

Then I had my hands at his throat. 'You maniac!' I snarled. 'You killed him!'

'He was going to cry out! I had to stop him!'

'You can't just kill—'

'Wake up!' Old Axel struggled free. 'This is not the world you used to know! This is the end times! Can you understand that?'

I fell back weakly. 'He didn't deserve that,' I said. 'He was just an old man.'

'And now he's a dead old man,' Old Axel said. 'But if you go back and change history then none of this will happen.' He pointed at the body. 'He'll lead a completely different life, free of the horror caused by James Price.'

The old man was so still. I stared down at his body. *Have you seen my wife? She left to buy flowers.* Now he was dead and we didn't even know his name.

'There will be no more killing,' I said. My

voice sounded like it belonged to someone else. 'You won't kill anyone else.'

'Change history and he won't die,' Old Axel said.

'You don't know that,' Ebony said. 'You don't know what an alternative future will hold.'

'It'll be better than this.'

He told us we needed to keep moving; a resistance cell nearby would help us.

'What about Chad and Brodie?' I asked.

'They're resourceful. We'll catch up with them later.'

What sort of answer is that? I wanted to punch him in the face, which was pretty funny, really, because it meant I wanted to punch myself. *What is his problem?* He made it sound like they were lost at Disneyland, not forty years in the future.

But he was right. Chad and Brodie *were* resourceful. They could survive just about anything.

Old Axel went to the back of the store. Pushing aside some shelving, he revealed a door. 'Looks like there's an exit through here.'

I couldn't believe we were leaving the old man here. *Does nobody get buried anymore?* My eyes scanned the counter. On it sat a dusty vase filled with plastic flowers. I placed them gently on the old man's chest.

'That's very touching,' Old Axel called out, 'but we—'

'Shut up!' I snapped. 'You may have lost your humanity, but I haven't.'

We followed Old Axel through the exit into an alley lined with rubbish. A year's worth of trash was here.

'This is disgusting,' Ebony said, screwing up her nose. 'Is the whole city like this?'

'Some of it's worse. At least we're in a livable section.'

'This is livable?'

'Walls enclose the habitable sections. Most of the planet's drowning in toxic gas.'

'So what went wrong?' I asked. 'How did we end up here?'

'The Agency had a lot of teething problems

59

with the development of the time machine. We're lucky we ended up here and not at the battle of Waterloo.'

Old Axel told us more about the badlands. Most of the major cities were protected by huge walls; outside them lay areas where the gas would kill you within hours. The mid-west was one huge storm, an out of control hurricane that had been active for over a decade. It even had a name. The Eye.

'What caused the gas?' I asked.

'Another one of Price's experiments,' Old Axel snorted. 'He had some insane idea about terraforming the planet into a new garden of Eden.'

Whatever James Price had done had messed up the world. Reaching the end of the alley, we hurried across an abandoned street. Before reaching the other side, I looked up and saw a poster of a man, fifty feet high, on the side of a building. The words below were old and rotting, but still readable:

The Agency is your friend

'Is that—' I started.

'James Price,' Old Axel confirmed. 'The years—and plastic surgery—have been kind. He doesn't look much different to that in your time.'

We started down another alley.

'How did all this happen?' Ebony asked. 'How did one man take over the Agency? And the world?'

'I can't say much for fear of contaminating the time line,' Old Axel said, 'but you should know that James Price is a genius. In terms of intellect, he's a Leonardo da Vinci or Albert Einstein. Unfortunately, unlike them, he is completely without morals. After joining the Agency, he became obsessed with controlling it, then the United States and finally the planet.'

We walked in silence. While I didn't agree with his murder of the old man, I was starting to understand my older self. His life had been unbearably hard. Our lives were difficult, but he had lived through the fall of civilization, the end of the world.

We descended to a disused subway, climbed over rusting gates and continued down another flight of stairs. The gloom grew worse by the minute; I wished we had torches. I was just about to suggest this when Old Axel stopped at an empty vending machine. He eased a corner of it aside and I heard him exchange a few words with someone.

'Come on,' he said, turning to us. 'We're here.'

He pushed the vending machine aside and a faint glow sprang from a hole behind. We passed the gatekeeper, a dirty looking woman with matted hair and one arm, and continued along an old section of subway. A string of faint LED lights hung from the walls. On both sides of the long defunct rail line, people sat, engaged in different sorts of work: repairing clothing, cleaning guns, cooking foods on oil burners.

Ebony shot a horrified look at me. Was this how people lived? In the darkness? With little hope of survival?

'For most people it's worse,' Old Axel said.

'Things would be better, but there's not much collaboration between the different branches of the rebellion.'

'Why?' I asked.

'There are traitors everywhere. Information dissemination is at a minimum. The less you know, the better, in case you're captured and tortured.' He grimaced. 'Mind you, it's different for Agency employees. They live in palatial accommodation in the city's red zones.'

'Red zones?'

'Closed compounds guarded by Agency security.'

Old Axel led us into the basement of a building. The only light was through a tiny window high on the wall, but I still felt relieved. Feeble daylight was better than none at all.

An old black man with gray hair, and a long scar down one side of his face, sat at a table. He had been studying a set of schematics, but now he turned, his mouth falling open in astonishment.

'I don't believe it,' he said. 'It's not possible.'

I stared at him blankly. *Who was he?*

'Mr. Brown!' Ebony cried, embracing him.

Mr. Brown. The man who had first trained me at the Agency. A man who was as much a friend as he was a mentor. Open mouthed, I shook his hand and then went in for the full hug. He glared at Old Axel.

'You weren't supposed to bring them back,' he said. 'Why'd you do that?'

'They were harder to convince than I expected.' He explained what had happened. 'So we've lost the time ship as well as the temporal resonators.'

'Chad and Brodie will probably get picked up by the resistance,' Mr. Brown said, thoughtfully. 'The real problem is getting you all back.'

'Back?' I said.

'To your own time. We've almost completed another time machine, but the big problem is the temporal resonator.' I must have looked astonished because he smiled slightly. 'The time machine is a complicated device, but is based on a perpetual energy device Price developed years ago. We've had access to those plans for years. The difficult part is the resonator. It contains a rare element called Francium.'

'You have contacts within the Agency?' I asked.

'Not everyone in the Agency is on board with their program. They leak information to us all the time.'

'So how do we get a temporal resonator?'

Mr. Brown smiled. 'Feel like a little excitement?'

Chapter Ten

'Whatever made us do this?' Brodie groaned. 'We had a nice tropical island to explore. Days of lying in the sun. We could've eaten coconuts till we puked.'

'The perfect life,' Chad agreed.

She and Chad were in the hallway of a derelict building where he had carried her after the red man had collapsed the building. By the time she had regained consciousness, the fight was over and armed security forces were roaming the streets.

Now we're lost forty years in the future, she thought. *And everyone wants to kill us.*

'I tried my wrist communicator,' Chad said. 'It's not working.'

'I'm not surprised. The Agency probably uses a dampening field to kill communications.' The city was a disaster zone. It seemed Old Axel had been telling the truth about the future. 'I wonder how we'll find the others.'

'There must be some sort of resistance

movement. We need to make contact.' Chad thought for a moment. 'Maybe we can put an ad on Craigslist.'

'I don't think—'

'Joking.'

'Okay.'

'I'm a funny guy, but what else would you expect from The Chad?' He stared at her. 'What?'

'There you go again. Spoiling everything.'

'How do you mean?'

She gently tapped his head. 'There might be a nice guy trapped under that inflated ego. You should let him out some time.'

Chad shrugged. 'We're superheroes. That makes us better than the average person.'

'I'm sure Hitler thought the same thing.'

'He didn't have super powers.'

'No-one's superior to anyone else,' Brodie said, patiently. 'Everyone deserves respect as long as they act decently.' She peered down the hallway. 'Let's get moving.'

They left through the rear of the building and

maneuvered down a thin alley choked with mounds of garbage. There was not a person to be seen, but Brodie had the feeling they were being watched.

I wouldn't come out either, she thought.

A flying ship, resembling a helicopter, but with the rotors removed, passed overhead and disappeared behind a building.

'There's still plenty of technology around,' Chad said.

'All owned by the Agency, I guess. Let's see where that ship went.'

They navigated an abandoned street clogged with a decades old traffic jam and continued up another alley. Reaching the end, they gazed out at a familiar landmark.

'Is this Times Square?' Chad asked.

'It *was* Times Square. Now it's just a mess.'

The once iconic area now lay in ruin. Some of the buildings had collapsed. The myriad of distinctive billboards were either broken or missing. A mammoth hole was at the corner of Broadway and West Forty-Seventh Street. The famous Toshiba billboard was long defunct. A huge canvas sign with an image of a smiling face hung over it. The wording beneath read:

Terrorists Will Be Shot

'I wonder if that's James Price,' Chad said.

'I bet it is,' Brodie said. 'What's going on with that ship?'

The rotor vessel hovered over the middle of the square where a pile of rubble lay. Both sides of the aircraft opened and military personnel spilled out on ropes and abseiled down. Finally a man with a hood over his head, and cuffed hands, was lowered to the ground. Two of the guards picked him up and attached him to a large stake in the center of the rubble.

'I don't like the look of this,' Chad muttered. 'It looks like they're going to execute that guy.'

One of the guards whipped the hood off the prisoner's head and the man stood blinking in the hot sun. He wore a thick collar around his neck, some sort of electronic device. His eyes settled on the nearest guard and he said something. The guard responded by punching him in the stomach. The man doubled over.

A guard pulled a device from his pocket and pressed a button. A chime rang out from the roofs of the shattered buildings.

'Samuel Taffe,' the guard said, his voice reverberating around the quiet streets. 'You have been found guilty of crimes against the Agency. These crimes include terrorism, theft of Agency property and the murder of Agency personnel.'

Incredibly, Samuel Taffe laughed in response and another of the guards stepped forward and backhanded him across the face.

'This is terrible,' Brodie said. 'They're going to kill him.'

'We can't do anything,' Chad said. 'We've got to look after ourselves.'

'At the cost of someone else's life?' Brodie spun on him. 'And you wonder why people don't respect you?'

'That's not fair,' Chad said, turning red. 'We're out of our depths.'

Brodie turned away from him and Chad fumed in silence.

Why does she have to be so pig-headed? They were outnumbered and outgunned. And neither of them was invincible. No-one with brains would take on these guys.

Except...

Except Axel. But then he was the big Kahuna of the group. Axel would come flying in like a superhero and save that guy.

But this isn't about Axel, Chad thought. *It's about me. Do I have what it takes?*

Do I?

The men stepped back from the makeshift stake, formed a line and raised their weapons.

Taking them on would be insane, Chad thought. *Completely insane.*

Chad stepped into the street.

Call me insane.

Chapter Eleven

'Excuse me,' he yelled. 'I'm looking for some directions.'

Fifty feet lay between him and the man they were about to execute. Chad waved in a friendly manner as he strode towards them. Turning at the sound of his voice, the men leveled their weapons.

'Stay where you are!' the leader commanded. 'This is Agency business!'

'I understand that,' Chad said, continuing. 'But I really need your help.'

Forty feet. A bead of sweat trailed down the side of Chad's face.

'Stop!' A guard yelled. 'That's an order!'

Chad kept walking. 'I'm so sorry. My hearing's not so good. I haven't been the same since someone dropped a building on me.'

Thirty feet.

A guard said to the leader, 'We had reports of unauthorized mods operating in the area.'

Twenty feet.

Their leader fired a warning shot. It pinged off the road in front of Chad and he stopped, raising his arms in surrender.

'I apologize,' he said. 'I didn't mean to cause any trouble. Someone shot me up with drugs a while back and turned me into a superhero.'

The leader aimed his weapon at Chad's head. 'Unauthorized mods are enemies of the Agency.'

'I've had issues with authority figures,' Chad explained. 'I think it's because I'm better than everyone else.'

Whatever the leader of the group was about to say was interrupted by the rock that slammed into the middle of his forehead, knocking him unconscious. The other men fell back in surprise.

Chad nodded to Brodie who stood in a nearby alley, dusting her hands with satisfaction. 'Nice shot!' he yelled.

'Thanks!'

Chad turned, raised his arm and fired blocks of ice at each of the armed men. He dove to one side as they opened fire. He rolled, their bullets narrowly missing him. He formed a wall of compressed ice. A hail of bullets started to demolish it.

Another guard fell as a rock struck his chest. Chad spent a micro-second admiring Brodie's abilities. She had the abilities of three grown men—including their visual acuity.

I'm never playing baseball against you, Chad thought.

He twisted again, firing a blast of intense heat at a guard. It knocked him flying. Chad shot a volley at the tail section of the rotor craft, severing it completely. The flying vessel immediately spun out of control, smashed into the sign hanging over the Toshiba billboard and exploded.

Good, he thought. *We needed a diversion.*

Advancing on Samuel Taffe, he threw up another ice barrier to keep the guards away before freeze drying the handcuffs, and breaking them off. A guard screamed into his radio for backup.

'Looks like it's gonna get crowded,' Chad said.

'Get this neck brace off me,' Taffe yelled. 'I

can get us out of here.'

Two more rotor craft swept along the city streets towards them. They would start firing at any second. Brodie took out the remaining guards, grabbed Chad's arm and pointed at a dozen guards pouring around a corner. 'We've got company!'

'Take this thing off!' Taffe said. 'Quickly!'

Brodie shot Chad a look, and gripped the brace with all her strength. It gave a grinding sound and broke off.

Samuel Taffe grabbed their arms. 'Hang on. This will be disorientating.'

'What will?' Chad asked.

Then Chad saw a nearby building fly towards him—or did he fly towards it? He passed through where a family lived deep within the structure. They were eating beans out of a can. Then he saw empty rooms. A dilapidated restaurant.

What the hell's going on?

Brodie and Taffe appeared to be the only stationery things in the universe. Everything else was rushing past them. Brodie's mouth was open in astonishment. Or was it horror?

They went through the rear wall of the building and continued along a street at super speed, passing wrecked cars, broken buildings, the remains of a crashed passenger jet. Chad saw them approach a homeless man. For one horrifying moment he thought they were going to crash into him, but then he was inside the man; he could see his blood vessels, his brain and the interior of his skull.

They continued on. Passed under a bridge. Across the murky sludge of what had once been the East River. Another building rushed at them—and they flew straight through it.

Suddenly they were passing streets filled with yellow fog. Chad tried to yell out, but he couldn't move, couldn't make a sound.

Samuel Taffe's power was teleportation. Unlike them, he was able to move, and now he shot a cheeky grin at Chad.

Glad you're enjoying yourself, Chad thought.

Taffe was right about one thing; it *was* disorientating. Chad felt like his stomach had been left back in Times Square. A terrible thought occurred to him. Maybe it had. Maybe something had gone wrong and part of his internal anatomy *was* missing.

What a horrible way to die, he thought. The Chad, the greatest superhero who had ever lived, strewn across New York City like a bag of trash. What would they say about him?

Here lies Chad. And here. And over here.

They slid through more buildings, now moving more slowly.

I feel sick, Chad thought. *I'm going to vomit. That might be a good sign. You can't vomit without a stomach.*

Can you?

The fog disappeared and they went past another building into what was once a park. The trees were dead, and the grass, dust. They slowed and came to a grinding stop. For a horrifying moment Chad thought the teleportation had failed because now he was frozen solid.

I'm gonna be like this forever—

Then he felt sun on his face and the world

snapped back to normal. They weren't in Times Square; he had no idea where they were. His feet hit the earth and he toppled over. He was dimly aware of Brodie hitting the ground nearby. Chad sucked in great lungfuls of air. He felt dizzy. And sick.

'That last bit is the worst,' Taffe said. 'I've got to create a perfect vacuum before we rematerialize. That means pushing all the atoms aside. If I didn't then you'd be sharing the same space with other matter. The result wouldn't be pretty.'

Chad struggled to his knees. He tried to speak, but then his stomach caught up with him and he started to heave.

'Don't feel too bad,' Taffe said. 'That happens to everyone.'

Chapter Twelve

It was Dan's belt buckle that saved him.

As the floor collapsed beneath him, Dan fell through the air, instinctively focusing on staying upright. His belt buckle jerked upwards, leaving him suspended in mid-air.

The crash of the collapsing floor seemed to echo forever. Finally, it subsided and Dan allowed himself to peep downwards. Dust was still everywhere, but the debris had settled. He slowly lowered himself to the remains of the floor below.

'Some superhero I am,' he muttered.

He was glad the others had not seen this. Chad would have laughed at him, and it would have confirmed to Axel and Brodie that he was too young to be part of the team. And Ebony—

Well, she always barracked for the underdog. She would have been on his side. He sighed. *Anyone* could have stepped onto that floor. He was alive. That's what mattered.

So now what? The floor had collapsed into

some kind of lab. Benches were everywhere, covered in chemistry equipment and papers. Most of them had been destroyed in the floor collapse, but some had survived. Dan climbed over the debris to one of the benches. The pages were old and dusty, and covered in writing.

He tapped his communicator and showed Ferdy one of the pages via the camera. 'This is Japanese,' Dan said. 'Right?'

'That's correct, Dan.'

'So the Japanese were here? Maybe during the war?'

'The history of this island shows no details about Japanese occupation.'

'Why do—' Dan stopped. 'Ferdy, can you hear that?'

Dan listened hard. A darkened corridor led away from this chamber. A murmur came from it.

'Ferdy cannot hear anything unusual,' Ferdy said, pausing. 'Groundhog Day is celebrated on the second of February—'

'I'll get back to you on that.' Dan

disconnected the link and peered down the corridor. He listened hard. He could hear a distant voice. Could someone else be here? A shiver tickled his spine. Could a Japanese soldier still be here from the war? He had heard stories of soldiers fighting long after its finish.

But he would be as old as a dinosaur if he had fought World War Two. Or dead. Or a ghost. And ghosts weren't real. Were they?

A faint light came from a skylight at the far end of the corridor.

'I'm a superhero,' Dan murmured. 'Some old ghost isn't going to scare me.'

He focused on a piece of steel pipe in the debris. It flew into his hand and he followed the corridor to a T-intersection. The voice was louder. On both sides of the corridor were cells, locked and empty, containing rotting bunks.

Dan sniffed. The smell down here was bad. Really bad. The mold had taken over years ago. It probably should have been the only living thing down here.

The sound had stopped.

Dan listened to the silence. Now he wasn't sure what was more unnerving; the voice or its absence. He swallowed hard as he tightly gripped the metal pipe. It felt slippery.

'Dan?'

Ferdy's voice shattered the silence.

'Yes! Ferdy!' Dan said. 'What do you want?'

'Ferdy had not heard from you for some time. It seemed prudent to check on your condition.'

'My condition is...fine. I'm investigating something down here.'

'Ferdy has some new information regarding the time ship.'

'What is it?'

'The *Liter8tor* picked up a transmission when the ship first arrived. The systems dismissed it as interference, but Ferdy has been able to determine it to be an encoded message.'

'And it says...?'

'Ferdy has been unable to determine its meaning.'

'You've got the most incredible brain in the universe and you can't decode it?'

'Ferdy is as surprised as you, friend Dan. Ferdy is possibly the most intelligent being to ever exist—'

'And the most modest.'

'—and yet the code is so advanced that even Ferdy is perplexed.' He paused. 'It can be solved, but only by knowing the correct encryption key.'

It all sounded very odd to Dan, but now the whispering had started again. Someone was speaking in English. It sounded like they were reading. Dan signed off and listened hard.

The skylight in the roof was broken, with vines growing into the building. The corridor led to darkness in one direction, the other to a single cell where the roof had caved in.

Dan headed in this direction, the sound growing louder. By the time he reached the end, he could make out a huge hole in the ceiling. The rubble below had formed a natural staircase into the cell. Vines and palm fronds covered the rubble.

A small boy was curled up on the moldy bunk with a book clasped firmly in his hand. Lowering it, he stared at Dan in amazement.

'I'm Henry,' the boy said. 'What are you?'

Chapter Thirteen

The resistance had been busy. I realized this the instant we entered the heart of the base, a huge underground chamber the size of a football field. A thousand people lived there in a makeshift shanty town, lit by banks of fluorescent lights set into the ceiling.

'We didn't build this, but we had to fix it up,' Mr. Brown explained.

'What is this place?' Ebony asked.

'We think it started off as a naturally occurring cavern,' Mr. Brown said. 'Then it looks like the government set it up as an underground shelter in case of nuclear attack.' He added, 'That must have been during the cold war.'

'And the Agency doesn't know about it?' I asked.

'We made certain all references to it were removed from Agency computers,' he said, smiling grimly. 'Like I said before, friends in high places.'

We crossed the cavern and I was reminded of

the compound in Las Vegas where we had been situated. I felt a tinge of loss. They hadn't been great times, but they hadn't been that bad either. You don't appreciate what you've got till you don't have it anymore.

'There isn't anywhere else you can hide?' I asked. Being anywhere near a major city seemed a bad idea.

'There probably are, but they don't hold a thousand people.'

'Why is James Price so intent on destroying the planet?'

'He wasn't always like this,' Old Axel spoke up. 'People welcomed his inventions in the beginning. They made life easier. He eventually became a techno hero. He seemed harmless enough, so the government gave him more power.'

'So what happened?'

'Under that geeky exterior was a psychotic interior. Price was willing to take terrible risks in the name of science.'

'Like what?'

'I can't say. It would—'

'Contaminate the time line. Yeah, I know.'

We entered another railway tunnel, colder here, the light weaker. I didn't notice the door at the end until we were almost on it. The next room was shaped like a huge cylinder and well lit. Pieces of machinery lay everywhere. Men with welding torches huddled around a vessel in the center. Power leads ran from it to a generator.

They were trying to disguise the ship, but I would have been blind to not recognize it.

'You've got to be kidding,' I said.

Liber8tor.

The years had not been kind to our old ship. The Tagaar warship had obviously been through a lot of battles. Sections of the hull, not disguised with new plating, were scarred and damaged. One support leg looked like it had been completely replaced.

A thought occurred to me. 'Ferdy,' I said. 'What's happened to—'

'Long gone,' Old Axel said. 'Price had him purged from the Agency computers years ago.' He shook his head. 'Don't ask.'

Ferdy. It was terrible, but I had not spared a thought for him since our arrival. So he was dead. Again. I wondered about James Price. Could killing one man really change the future of world history?

'What are you doing to *Liber8tor*?' Ebony asked.

'We're getting her ready for our mission. The old girl is not what she was, but she's still able to get past Agency radar and into orbit.'

'Orbit?'

He nodded. 'The Agency's main research facility—*Olympus*—is in orbit. We have access codes that'll get us past security.'

I nodded at the new panels. 'What's with the disguise?'

Mr. Brown spoke up. 'It's highly unlikely that anyone is actually going to look out an *Olympus* window, but if they do they should see something that looks like an Agency vessel. Kind of.'

'And who's the pilot?' I asked.

'I am,' Mr. Brown said. 'For this you get the

best.'

I felt a little better about the mission. He led us to quarters that looked more like a cell than a residence, but as least they were clean, containing two bunk beds and a bench. Meals arrived a few minutes later, stew made of a fine meat. Mr. Brown said it was rabbit, but I kept thinking about the rats I'd seen in the upper tunnels.

I ate it anyway.

Mr. Brown stopped at the door just before he left. 'It's nice to see you again,' he said, his eyes misting over. 'It's so good to see you young...and strong and healthy. I've missed the old days. I've missed them a lot.'

'Thanks,' I said. 'For everything.'

Nodding, he pulled the door shut behind him. I turned off the light as we climbed into our bunks and stared at the black ceiling. 'It's been quite a day,' I said. We woke up this morning in the present and now we were forty years in the future. 'And the worst part is that I'm a douche bag.'

'You're not a douche bag,' Ebony said. 'Your

future self is, but...I mean...'

'I get your drift. I think.'

'You're not like him at all. But this is a different world. I can see why he...you...want James Price dead.' She sighed. 'What should we do?'

'About what?'

'About James Price.'

I had already been through this once. I had been given the choice to sentence the Russian Premier to an equally terrible fate—and I hadn't been able to pull the trigger. But this was worse. The fate of the entire human race could depend on us.

'I don't know,' I said. 'What do you think?'

But Ebony didn't answer. She was already asleep.

Chapter Fourteen

What are you? Dan thought. *What sort of question is that?*

'Uh, hello,' Dan said, flustered. 'What am I? I'm a boy like you.'

'I'm a boy like you,' Henry said.

'How did you get here?' Dan asked.

'How did you get here?'

He's just repeating everything I say, Dan thought.

'I arrived in a plane,' he said.

'I arrived in a plane.'

'Do you understand what I'm saying?' Dan asked. 'Are you here with your family? Or are you alone?'

'Alone.' Henry looked at the ceiling. 'That is day.'

It was worse than having a conversation with Ferdy. At least Ferdy made sense. Maybe Henry suffered from an intellectual disability. But how did he get here? Were there others with him? Dan tapped his communicator.

'Ferdy? I've found a boy in the basement of the building.' The only reply was a long squeal of static. 'Can you hear me, Ferdy?'

Nothing. There was a problem with reception. Dan pretended to examine the cell lock.

'I think this is broken,' he said, gripping it in his hand, but focusing on the metal. It snapped open. 'At least I can get you out of there. Where are your parents?'

'No parents.' Henry's voice was soft. He had wide, brown eyes and black hair, and wore trousers, black shoes and a white open necked shirt. He was surprisingly clean considering the state of the cell. 'My name is Henry.'

'I'm Dan.'

'Dan.'

Dan's eyes followed the trail of debris leading to the opening. Thick jungle surrounded the top.

'Will you follow me?' Dan asked.

The boy regarded Dan uncertainly for a moment before trailing him outside. A fresh breeze pushed back Dan's hair. It was cooler. Maybe the weather was changing.

Henry still held the book.

'Is that good?' Dan asked.

'Reading.'

'Is it good?'

'Good.'

Dan sighed. This was a terribly one sided conversation. Still, at least Henry seemed able to read. Dan glanced at the cover of the novel. *Doctor Jekyll and Mr Hyde*. Hardly a bedtime story, but maybe it was the only book he owned.

Activating his communicator, this time Ferdy's voice came back loud and clear. He explained finding Henry. 'Are there any records of shipwrecks in this area?' he asked.

'A sailing ship called the *Morning Star* went missing in this area ten years ago.'

'Who was on board?'

'A family of four. John and Carla Benson and their boys Phillip and Charles.'

Dan turned to Henry. 'Do the names Charles

and Phillip mean anything to you?' he asked, gently.

Henry shook his head.

'Ferdy, how old were those boys?'

'Charles was seven. Phillip was two.'

Phillip could really be Henry, but why wouldn't he know his own name?

Henry pointed towards the coast. 'Ship,' he said. 'Beach.'

Dan led the boy towards the beach along an overgrown path. A bird cried out and went crashing through the trees. Stepping onto the sand, Dan felt both relief and sadness. He was glad to be free of the jungle, but he wished the others were here.

The beach curved for miles in both directions. This island could have been a Mecca for tourists except it was a long way from anywhere. A white and angular shape poked from the jungle—the stern of a boat.

Drawing near, Dan saw it was a sailing vessel about thirty feet in length. Once it was a beautiful ship, but now its mast was gone and half of the vessel lay buried in the sand.

Dan wiped grime off the stern.

'*Morning Star*,' he read. 'Henry, is this your ship?'

The boy stared at him blankly.

'Henry, did you come here on this ship?' Dan persisted. 'With your brother and your parents?'

The boy said nothing. He looked back into the jungle and, for the first time, an expression of fear twisted his face.

'Henry, what is it?'

'There's a monster,' he said. 'It comes out at night.'

'I can fight off monsters,' Dan assured him. 'I'll be back soon.'

He climbed on board the buried ship. It arrowed into the sand at a thirty degree angle. Some of the ropes that had once been attached to the sail still remained, but they were hopelessly tangled and rotten. Dan found a hatch halfway down the deck. He tried moving it by hand. Stuck. He applied his powers and it slid back with a painful screech.

A sound came from below deck.

Dan frowned. It had sounded like the shuffle of feet. 'I'm a superhero,' he muttered. 'I can take on ten villains at once.'

But he still felt afraid.

He climbed into what was once a classy living room, but now it had been wrecked by the elements. It smelt of mildew. A lounge ran along the port side, but the fabric had rotted. A few old magazines lay in a pool of water. Timber peeled from the coffee table in the center.

A hallway led to the bridge, a hole in the hull and jungle beyond. Dan crept towards the stern.

The first room contained four bunk beds. Some old children's toys were on the floor but, like everything else on board, these were ruined. He continued down the hall until he reached the next room, the door jammed half-open. It seemed that more refuse was scattered across the floor, but then Dan spotted the human skull.

He grimly examined the remains. There were two bodies. Adults by the look of it. Probably the remains of John and Carla Benson. Their ruined clothing was mixed among the mishmash pile of bones.

From the stern came another sound. Footfalls on the wooden decking. Dan edged to the doorway. He used his mind to pick up a rusty crossbeam from the floor. Anyone—or anything—had better watch out if they tried to take him down!

I'm a superhero, he told himself. *I have amazing powers. I can lift up tons of metal and throw it at bad guys.*

I'm Metal Boy, he thought.

He liked the sound of that. Metal Boy.

Henry had mentioned a monster on the island, but monsters weren't real.

Were they?

He peered into the hallway. He couldn't see anything, but he was sure he could hear breathing. It couldn't be Henry. He was still outside and the breathing was too guttural anyway. Dan stepped out cautiously, the piece of metal floating in the air next to him. It was dark here and there was still no sign—

Something crashed into his legs, sending Dan

flying. He heard a wild grunting and a squeal. The metal beam fell onto his head. Yelling, he spun about in horror as a hairy, brown creature bolted past him and out of sight.

A pig! That's all it was. Some sort of wild boar. The creature must have been rooting about in the broken remains of the ship. He remembered hearing that early sailors would often leave pigs on remote islands so there would be fresh meat for them when they later returned.

Dan felt a flush of embarrassment. What sort of superhero was he? A wild pig just scared him half to death! He swallowed hard. Henry probably heard the racket and was wondering what was happening.

He returned to the upper deck, but Henry was gone. Dan crossed to the edge of the water. From here he could see up and down the coast.

'Henry!' he called. 'Where are you?'

Silence. Then the roar of a beast rang out from deep inside the jungle. It wasn't the snort of a wild boar. It wasn't like anything that Dan had ever heard in his life. A flock of birds broke cover and sailed away towards the setting sun.

What had Henry told him?

There's a monster and it comes at night.

Chapter Fifteen

'There it is,' Mr. Brown said. '*Olympus*.'

Ebony and I were sitting on *Liber8tor*'s bridge. It was surprisingly clean although quite different to the *Liber8tor* we knew. Most of the reptilian Tagaar consoles had been removed and replaced with sleek stainless steel panels, and someone had whitewashed the walls, a strange thing to do to an alien spacecraft, but these were strange times.

Old Axel had gone below to check a shudder in the engines while Mr. Brown controlled the helm. It was strange seeing him there instead of Dan. I wanted to ask him what had happened to Dan and the others over the years, but I was sure he would give the same answer as Old Axel.

It would cause irreparable damage to the space/time continuum.

The space station known as *Olympus* filled the view screen. Covered in green metal, it was shaped like a giant donut with a one-eighth section cut out.

Cannons ringed the circumference. The size of it was hard to determine at first, but then I spotted a ship entering one of the cut ends of the donut. *Olympus* was massive. Miles across.

'How on Earth did something like that get built?' I asked.

'I can't say much because it—'

'I know. Space/time continuum. I get the idea.'

'Suffice to say, James Price was able to lasso a passing asteroid and transform it with nanites into a space station.

'You're kidding.'

'I wish I were.'

Nanites were tiny machines only a few atoms in size. They were already being used in some basic applications in our time, but it sounded like they had been fully exploited by James Price and the Agency.

Mr. Brown continued. 'After the station was completed—'

'Shut up,' Old Axel said, appearing in the doorway with a box. 'You know better than to blab.'

Mr. Brown clamped his mouth shut. 'Just giving them some warning. That's all.'

'They less they know the better.' He glared at me. 'The things I could say would make your blood boil.'

I stared back. There was a terrible darkness in him, a deep hurt that had twisted him into something unrecognizable. *Were we really the same person?*

Old Axel produced belts with holsters attached. 'I've got these for everyone,' he said. 'They're simple laser pistols. You just point and shoot.'

'We don't normally use guns,' Ebony said.

'You might need them this time. This base hasn't been attacked by mods for over a decade, but they could have zeno emitters installed.'

Zeno emitters could render our powers completely useless. I didn't like our chances of surviving this without superpowers. I wished Brodie was with us. She was the only one of us zeno emitters couldn't affect.

'Thinking about Brodie?' Old Axel asked me.

Maybe I was wearing a crazy grin. 'Yes.'

'Don't,' he said, his face black. 'Stay focused on the mission. We'll be lucky to make it out alive.'

The space station grew larger. I swallowed. Not only was *Olympus* massive, but probably protected to the gills. By comparison, there were four of us. How were we going to win against such odds?

'Cold feet?' Old Axel grinned.

He was reading my mind, or his mind, as it happened.

'No.'

'This all could have been avoided. I begged you to kill James Price, but you wanted evidence. Well, now you've got it.'

I couldn't argue with him there. The future was obviously a terrible place and it seemed James Price was responsible for it. Killing him would be like killing Hitler. No-one would blame you for killing Hitler. If you could make the world into a better place—a *much* better place—wouldn't you?

'We're reaching R1,' Mr. Brown said. 'I'm sending the recognition codes.'

'What's R1?' Ebony asked.

'A security checkpoint. This is the first.'

Continuing towards a blunt end of the station, I saw a space dock with several ships moored inside. Ringing the outside were a dozen cannons aimed in our direction.

'Fortunately for us,' Old Axel said, 'the research lab containing the temporal resonators is only half-a-mile from this end. And I've got a map.'

'Providing we don't get blown up first,' Ebony said.

'They're returning our codes and allowing us through,' Mr. Brown said.

I let out a sigh of relief.

'Don't get too cocky,' Old Axel said. 'That's only the first checkpoint. There are two others to go.'

The space port filled the entire view screen. I remembered the extra plating that had been used to disguise *Liber8tor*. What if someone looked out the window and saw it wasn't an Agency ship?

'We've reached R2,' Mr. Brown said. 'I'm sending the second codes.'

My throat was dry. I glanced down at my hands. I was sweating. Usually I was able to control my fear, but that was when I was in control of the situation. Here I wasn't. I was decades in the future on a ship that might get blown to pieces at any second. I glanced at Ebony. She was pale.

For some terrible reason, this made me feel better. I tried to give her a reassuring smile, but it probably looked more like a grimace.

'They're not returning our codes,' Mr. Brown said.

I wondered what I would do if they fired on us. Maybe I could create an air pocket around us if the ship was blasted apart. That would temporarily save us, but how would we get onto the station? A throbbing pain started at the back of my neck. This was suicide. What were we doing here? Surely there was another way to get a temporal resonator? I was about to speak when Mr. Brown let out a sigh of relief.

'They've sent back the confirmation signal. We're safe.'

'One more checkpoint,' Old Axel said.

Liber8tor accelerated. 'Sending the final codes,' he said. 'This is it.'

I rubbed my neck, glancing at Ebony. Her eyes were closed. What was she doing? Oh, praying. I sent up a message as the ship entered the space dock. The ship shuddered as artificial gravity took over. We were inside a massive airlock, with vessels all around us, many similar to our modified *Liber8tor*.

The docking port was only a few hundred feet away.

'I'm not getting a reply code,' Mr. Brown said, staring at his console. 'I don't like the look of this.'

'Don't panic,' Old Axel said. 'We've gotten this far.'

'Wait a second!' Mr. Brown's voice rose in panic. 'They're fixing cannons on us.'

'Raise the force field!' Old Axel snapped.

I heard the shimmer of the force field embracing the ship. An instant later something slammed into *Liber8tor* and we were thrown sideways. Old Axel swore as I desperately tried to focus on my plan to make an air pocket.

'Full throttle!' Old Axel yelled. 'Fire forward torpedoes!'

I felt the sudden surge of engines as the docking bay rushed towards us. Two torpedoes flew from us as cannon fire slammed into *Liber8tor* from all sides. Ebony screamed. Our missiles slammed into the interior doors of the docking bay, reducing them to scrap. Beyond lay a huge tunnel, large enough to hold our ship. We flew through the shattered remains of the doors.

'Fire torpedoes!' Old Axel screamed.

Two more torpedoes rushed away from us. Another explosion followed. The view screen dissolved into static and *Liber8tor* crashed into the space station, catapulting me onto the floor.

After that, I knew nothing.

Chapter Sixteen

'That was quite a ride,' Chad said.

He had finished vomiting and was now shakily on his feet. Brodie had suffered a similar reaction from the transportation. She said to Taffe, 'That's quite an ability you've got there.'

'Thanks.' He motioned to a half-demolished building. 'We have to take cover,' he said. 'Agency forces regularly patrol this area.'

They took shelter in the collapsed building. 'So where the hell are we?' Brodie said. 'It seemed like we traveled miles.'

'We did. We're in Queens. Or what's left of it.' His eyes narrowed. 'You're not from around here, are you?'

'How can you tell?'

'You look too well fed. The only people that look as healthy as you are Agency operatives.'

'We certainly don't work for the Agency.' Brodie briefly explained what had brought them here. She expected Taffe to laugh in disbelief, but he merely nodded.

'I heard the Agency was developing a time machine,' he said. 'Looks like James Price finally pulled it off.'

Chad asked, 'Is he as bad as everyone makes out?'

'Worse. If you get a chance to change history, do it. You'll be doing everyone a favor.'

'We really need to get back to Manhattan. Can you take us there?'

Taffe shook his head ruefully. 'I wish I could, but I have a serious limitation on my power. It takes me a week to recharge after I've teleported. If you don't mind waiting...'

Chad said to Brodie, 'We can't wait a week.'

'We've got to track down the others,' she said.

'I have some friends in the resistance,' Taffe said. 'They can point you in the right direction.'

Brodie and Chad followed Taffe down a narrow street into a shattered building. He knew the area well. They navigated to the back where a piece of iron lay across scattered debris. Pulling it aside,

Taffe led them down a set of stairs.

Brodie found herself blinking in the darkness. She could make out a basement with wine racks stacked to one side.

'Who's there?' a voice called from the gloom.

'It's Taffe. I've brought some people. We want to see Ellen.'

They heard the click of a gun being cocked. 'Raise your hands and prepare to be searched.'

Two men separated from the darkness and searched them. Brodie felt a little uncomfortable, but remained silent. This wasn't their world. After the men allowed them to pass, they continued down another flight of stairs into an underground car park. Some vehicles were still parked there, but looked like they hadn't been used in decades. Among them people sat cooking meals over small stoves, and cleaning weapons.

They weaved up more stairs to a gloomy room with windows boarded up on one side. A skinny woman, aged fifty, sat behind a desk.

Her eyes narrowed. 'Taffe,' she said, her

voice surprisingly deep. 'I heard you were taken by the Agency.'

'I was.' He introduced everyone. 'I got free thanks to these good people.'

'Lucky you,' Ellen said, dourly. 'I thought you'd been slated for execution.' Her eyes shifted to Chad and Brodie. 'How'd they get you free?'

'We've got some tricks of our own,' Chad said, producing a ball of fire in one hand and snow in the other. 'We're friends.'

'I'm sure you are,' Ellen said, looking completely unimpressed. 'How do we know you're not Agency spies?'

'Because we're not,' Brodie said. 'We need to get back to Manhattan. We have people waiting for us.'

Ellen gave a hollow laugh. 'You'll have to excuse me if I don't believe you.' She nodded to a space behind them. For the first time, Brodie saw people seated on torn lounge chairs around a table in the gloom. 'We've got to test you.'

'We're not looking for trouble,' Chad said,

creating a circle of fire around him and Brodie. 'We just need your help.'

The people stood up. They were blond, a brother and sister. One side of the girl's face was terribly scarred; the letter T had been burnt into it. 'Everyone needs help these days,' she said. 'It's that kind of world.'

'We don't want to hurt you,' Chad said.

'You won't,' the girl replied.

Chad's circle of fire disappeared. He tried to make it reappear, but nothing happened. 'How'd you do that?' he asked. 'Only a zeno emitter—'

The girl introduced herself as Sharla, and her brother as Drake. 'You're not the only one with powers,' Sharla smiled thinly. 'Not only am I a human zeno emitter, but I can also get the truth out of people.'

'We don't have anything to hide,' Brodie said, clenching her fists.

'Good,' Drake said. 'Then it'll be easy.'

The girl raised her hand and Brodie felt her eyes closing. She struggled to keep them open, but she felt as if she had not slept for a year.

When she opened her eyes next, she was floating on a raft on a black ocean. The sky was pitch black except for starlight from constellations unfamiliar to her. It was cool and quiet upon the ocean, but then she felt warmth on her back. Turning, she saw the sun rising on the horizon, except it wasn't the sun. It was an enormous eye and it could see—

'Brodie? Can you hear me?'

Brodie awoke. Chad was shaking her shoulder.

'I hear you,' she said, sitting up. She was on a lounge in the darkened room. Apart from Chad, only Ellen and Sharla remained. They were speaking quietly together at Ellen's desk. 'What happened?'

'I think Sharla can read minds,' Chad explained. 'Whatever they found in ours made them very excited.'

Ellen and Sharla finished their conversation.

'I apologize for the inconvenience,' Ellen said to Chad and Brodie.

'No problem,' Chad said. 'Nothing I love

better than getting brain probed.'

Sharla smiled without humor. 'Just be glad I was nice about it,' she said. 'Sometimes I'm not.'

'We understand the importance of your mission,' Ellen said. 'Sharla will take you back to Manhattan.'

Chad and Brodie both breathed a sigh of relief.

'But I should warn you,' Sharla said, 'we've got to cross the badlands.'

'And that's difficult?' Chad asked.

'It'll make everything else you've ever been though look like a walk in the park.'

Chapter Seventeen

I woke to the blaring of a siren in my ears and someone shaking my shoulder. 'Come on!' a voice growled. 'We've got to keep moving.'

I felt like a bus had landed on my head, but somehow I got to my feet, completely disoriented. Then I remembered. Time Travel. Forty years in the future. Temporal resonator. Ebony—

She climbed over a pile of shattered machinery towards me. The crash had completely destroyed *Liber8tor*. Gaping holes in the bulk head showed a corridor beyond.

'Security will be here any minute,' Old Axel said, dragging me towards the exit.

'Mr. Brown?' His motionless body was slumped over the console. 'Is he—?'

'Dead. Let's go.'

Then we were outside the ship and in a corridor. Broken metal lay everywhere. So did the bodies of several security guards. Old Axel checked his map and pointed ahead.

'This way!' he snapped. 'Double time.'

Old Axel pulled a device from his side pouch. It resembled a memory stick, but larger. He approached a nearby computer and placed it to the screen. It gave a loud click and the image turned to static.

'I'm glad that worked,' he said. 'It just changed this mission from impossible to barely survivable.'

'What is that?' I asked.

'A scrambler virus. It was devised by the Agency some years ago. It'll disrupt communications across the station for the next hour.'

We ran down the corridor. Glancing back to the ship, I thought about Mr. Brown. I couldn't believe we were just leaving him behind.

'Mr. Brown—' I began.

'You want to bring him as a good luck charm?' Old Axel grabbed the front of my shirt and slapped me hard across the face. 'Listen to me! You must both follow every direction I give or we'll die here! Do you understand?'

We nodded dumbly. He was right. Our chances of survival were almost zero, and we couldn't do anything to help Mr. Brown anyway. We reached a doorway that led to the next section as security guards appeared in the corridor ahead.

'Ebony!' Old Axel yelled, pointing at the floor. 'Oxygen!'

The floor beneath the security team dissolved and they fell as one to the level below. There was a sickening thud as they crashed, followed by screams of pain.

My future self grabbed me. 'Fly us across to the opposite door.'

I created a flying wing out of compressed air and got us across. Old Axel closed the door behind us. 'Turn this door to titanium,' he told Ebony.

She looked puzzled, but complied. Old Axel produced a small box from his pocket. 'Hold onto your hats,' he said, smiling.

He pushed the button. An instant later we heard a *wumpf*, the entire station shook and we were thrown to the floor. A new alarm started as Old Axel dragged us to our feet.

'What the hell was that?' I asked.

'A nuclear device I installed on *Liber8tor*.'

'A what?'

'It'll keep the Agency forces busy for a while.'

I stared in horror at the titanium wall. If it hadn't held—

'Let's go!'

Another team of guards came charging out of a side passage and I knocked them out with a blast of air. We turned down a side corridor where another two guards appeared. Before I could react, Old Axel had shot them both in the chest, killing them instantly.

I'm a monster, I thought. *This world has turned me into a monster.*

We turned another corner and this time doors opened on both sides of the passage. This was all happening so fast. I couldn't focus. Couldn't concentrate. Guards charged through with guns raised and Old Axel shot them.

He stopped to consult his map. 'This is it,' he said. 'We need to go up a floor.'

Looking upwards, I created a cyclone of air that I slammed into the ceiling. It dented—but held.

'Again!' Old Axel yelled.

I fought back an angry retort. I wanted to smash *him*. Instead I focused, driving the hurricane force into the ceiling again. After three more attempts, a crack appeared and we stepped back as green liquid dripped down.

'Take us up,' Old Axel ordered.

I didn't bother to argue. I levitated us through the hole and entered a chamber more like a swamp than a room on a space station. Trees, vines and parasitic plants were everywhere. Dirt and muddy pools covered the floor. A rotten egg smell choked the air. Moss grew across the ceiling. The only illumination was the glow of the purple ceiling.

'My God,' I said. 'Where the hell are we?'

'The biological experimentation centre,' Old Axel explained. 'We're almost there. We've only got one final obstacle to overcome.'

A scream came from something behind me and was hit by the stench of putrefying flesh. I saw a mighty tree stretching from floor to ceiling.

Something appeared from behind it. Something with a multitude of eyes...

Chapter Eighteen

'It's called the Hydra,' Old Axel said.

'How nice,' Ebony gulped, her eyes like full moons in the purple light. 'It has a name.'

The Hydra was the size and shape of a small house, with blue-green scales covering most of its body. Supporting it were four stumpy legs that ended in clawed feet. It had a dozen tentacles about ten feet long. Suckers, similar to those of an octopus, covered every inch of them. Each sucker was ringed by spikes; a single swipe would cut a person in two.

Scattered, seemingly at random across the length of the creature, were hundreds of red eyes, tinged with green. It the midst of this madness lay a mouth, a jagged rip that contained a double row of sharp teeth.

But possibly the most disgusting thing about the creature was its lips. They were strangely human, almost delicate.

I wondered how best to attack the monster. A burst of air would drive it back. Then maybe Ebony could create a steel blade—

Old Axel raised his gun and pulled the trigger. A single laser beam cut through the Hydra. It shuddered, its eyes opening in shock—and died.

What the—?

'That's it?' I said. 'It's *dead*?'

'I said it was the final obstacle,' Old Axel said. 'I didn't say it would be hard to kill.'

Ebony laughed, but it was flavored with hysteria.

Old Axel consulted the map as we crossed the swamp. Glancing back at the dead creature, I shivered as I remembered its eyes, tentacles, lips...

'Oh no,' I said. 'That creature...don't tell me it's...'

'Human? It was—once.'

Ebony's mouth dropped open. 'It was a person? What the—'

'Just be glad he's dead,' Old Axel advised. 'For all our sakes.'

Reaching a slime covered wall, he told me to make a hole. Seconds later we climbed into a pristine corridor, sucking in lungfuls of fresh air.

'Ebony,' Old Axel said. 'Turn the floor of the biological chamber to oxygen.'

That would cause the entire swamp, including the Hydra to drop to the floor below.

'Won't that crush—'

'—anyone beneath it. Yes,' Old Axel said, 'that's the idea.'

Ebony looked like she wanted to argue, but Old Axel's instructions had helped us to survive this long. Ebony knelt and reached for the floor.

She stood. 'No,' she said. 'I'm not doing it.'

Old Axel looked furious. 'This is—'

'Let's go,' she said. 'Let's just get these temporal...thingies...and get out of here.'

We continued down the corridor. The door at the end slid open and we entered a workshop with computer parts cramming the benches. Old Axel's eyes scanned the room until he focused on a door set into the wall. I opened it by expanding the molecules of air in the lock. It swung free.

'Bingo,' Old Axel said. Pieces of equipment

filled the shelves. He shook his head sadly. 'Some of these weapons would give the resistance such an advantage...' Checking two cases, he found the same devices we had seen on the time machine. 'Still, if this works we'll never have to worry about the Agency again.'

He handed a bag to me before snatching a beehive-shaped device off the shelf.

'This'll come in handy,' he said. 'Let's go.'

I glanced at a computer terminal and saw it was still filled with static. The communications systems were still scrambled. Rounding a bend, we entered a room with a metal pad in the center of the floor. Three men worked at consoles. Old Axel started firing at them.

'No!' I yelled.

But I was too late. Within seconds they were dead. I felt like grabbing my older self and shaking him, but there was no time. He read one of the consoles.

'Good.' He tapped a few keys. 'This is going to work.'

'What is?' Ebony asked, looking sick.

'These are transportation mats. They can be used for short range teleportation.'

'Teleportation?' I said. 'You've got to be kidding.'

'I told you James Price was brilliant. Get on the mat.'

We climbed onto the metal platform while Old Axel manipulated the controls. He pushed a button and the platform began to hum. Taking a running jump, he landed next to me—

—just as everything started to shimmer. The world divided into cubes. Then they divided into smaller cubes. And again. They continued to subdivide. I couldn't move. White light surrounded me. Then I saw tiny cubes reassembling into small cubes. Larger cubes. Blocks.

Except now we were standing on a metal mat in a completely different place, a maintenance area surrounded by vessels. A man worked on a landing strut. I knocked him out with a bolt of air before Old Axel could kill him.

Adjusting the beehive shaped device he had stolen from the vault, Old Axel set it on the matter transporter. He activated the transporter and the device disappeared.

'That should keep them busy.' We raced up the stairs of a fighter craft. Five times the size of an Earth fighter, I was seriously impressed, but we had no time to appreciate it. We scrambled onto the flight deck where Old Axel slid behind the controls.

'How can you operate all this technology?' I asked.

'Correspondence course,' he said, starting the engines. 'You remember I said we've had information leaking from the Agency for years. I've studied every schematic I could lay my hands on. Besides,' the vessel lifted off the ground, 'this ship isn't so different to the old flex craft. It's just larger.'

The entire station shuddered as we heard the distant rumble of an explosion. Old Axel gave a satisfied grunt. 'Right on time.' He aimed us at the nearest bulkhead. 'Let's hope the weapons are operational.' He flipped a switch, a missile roared away from us and the wall exploded into shrapnel.

Atmosphere erupting through the gap, we entered the void of space, the Earth beneath us. As Old Axel poured on the acceleration, I looked back at the space station. The space dock at one end was ruined. Another segment was open to space. It looked like the station was about to break apart. Bodies and pieces of metal were being blasted into the vacuum of space.

I felt sick. Slumping into my seat, I tried not to think of the multitude of people we had just killed.

'We did it,' Ebony said, collapsing next to me. 'We're alive.'

Old Axel shot me a rare smile. 'We're a resourceful person,' he said. 'Those who have wronged us will live to regret it.'

Whatever that meant.

Chapter Nineteen

Brodie peered up at the old sewer hatch. She, Chad and Sharla stood at the base of a rusty ladder dressed in protective suits; brown plastic outfits with helmets that looked disturbingly like goldfish bowls. The helmets contained miniature transmitters so they could communicate with each other.

'Every remaining habitable area on the planet is surrounded by walls hundreds of feet high,' Sharla explained. 'The gas in the badlands won't kill you immediately, but prolonged exposure will.'

'How were the badlands made?' Brodie asked.

'An experiment of James Prices that went horribly wrong. Now we're locked inside the walls like rats in a cage.'

Sharla handed them handguns that fitted neatly into holsters sewn into the suits. 'Try not to waste bullets,' she said. 'They're a precious commodity around here.'

'Why do we need guns?' Brodie asked.

'There are things living in the fog. They used

to be people. Somehow they've survived the gas...but what they've become isn't pretty.' She grimaced. 'And James Price dumps his biological experiments in the badlands.'

'Wonderful.'

'But the biggest issue is still the fog.'

'So if our suit rips..?'

'Don't breathe in. The fog contains an acidic compound. It will irritate human flesh, but breathing it in will burn your lungs. You could probably survive a few days without a suit. Not much more.'

'There isn't a way around?' Chad asked. 'Or under. Or over?'

'The subway tunnels have all been severed from here to Manhattan. If we had a vessel, you could try flying over the fog, but you'd show up on the Agency's tracking systems.' She paused. 'They'd shoot you out of the sky. It's this way or no way.'

Sharla climbed up the ladder first. She struggled with the hatch for a moment before it groaned open. Toxic gas started to pour into the tunnel. They quickly left, shutting the hatch behind them.

The mist was nicotine colored, and floated around them in tight, swirling formations. Sometimes, Brodie could see several feet ahead, but otherwise it was an impenetrable barrier. They were standing in a suburban street populated with closely set houses topped with pitched roofs. Brodie saw the distant sun. It dotted the sky like a brown rock in a murky river. She turned to Chad. Even he looked shocked.

'How often have you done this journey?' Brodie asked Sharla.

'About half a dozen times.'

'And you've always gotten through?'

'I've gotten through, but the people I've chaperoned haven't always been so lucky.'

'Why?'

'Because they didn't listen to me,' she said firmly, her eyes turning away as she remembered some distant tragedy. 'Follow my instructions and we'll be fine.'

She started down the street. Brodie was pretty certain she could survive anything that came at them.

She still had her abilities, suit or no suit. Chad, however, was locked inside his outfit; his powers wouldn't work outside it. Sharla, of course, had her powers, but they were probably ineffective as well. She seemed to have an instinctive ability to move quietly through the shifting haze, darting across the uneven ground with ease. Brodie felt like a blundering idiot by comparison. The suit was cumbersome, and the gun at her side made her feel unbalanced. Chad was close behind. He was quieter than usual. Possibly it was the seriousness of the situation. He was almost likable when he wasn't so full of himself.

They crossed a park. Amazingly, the grass and the trees were still alive, but matted with brown tar. Some of the trees seemed to be mutating to deal with the unnatural environment; their branches were anchored into the ground, as if seeking nourishment from the earth.

The fog cleared briefly, revealing a line of posters pasted across a wall, showing James Price with the message, *Report Terrorists to the Agency,* written across the bottom. An enterprising young rebel had responded by spray-painting swear words over them.

Sharla led them into a street where a pitched battle had been fought decades before; a school bus lay on its side with cars parked at each end to close the street off to traffic. Bullet holes riddled the makeshift barrier from one end to the other with skeletal remains scattered around the ground.

Brodie picked up a gun. It appeared intact.

'Leave it,' Sharla said quietly.

Without asking why, she put it down.

Reaching a corner, Sharla held up her hand. *Stop.* Brodie peered into the mist. She couldn't see anything. It continued to shift and flow around them like ghosts.

Then she saw Chad ready his weapon as a slithering sound echoed down the street. *What's causing it?* She saw a car creeping along the middle of the road.

No, not a car, but something as big.

It resembled an enormous armadillo. Its head

was short and stumpy with two horns at the front. One eye was shut; it had either been destroyed by the fog or in a battle with something else. The other eye was fixed on the road ahead.

The creature moved on a row of tiny feet like an enormous caterpillar, its rear ending in a long snake-like tail. It opened its mouth as if yawning and Brodie saw a jagged row of bottom teeth.

Sharla didn't seem in a hurry to escape, so Brodie guessed she intended to keep them here, still and silent. There could be dozens—or hundreds—of these things in the fog. Maybe it was best to avoid them completely. The creature slithered close to them.

Only a few more feet, Brodie thought. *It'll be past us and everything will be fine.*

Which would have been the case, but Chad chose that moment to fire his weapon into the ground.

Chapter Twenty

Chad let out a cry. 'I didn't mean to do that!' he yelled. 'It went off—'

The creature roared, whirling about in the mist, its single good eye narrowing on them. The creature's tail whipped about like a lasso and flew towards Sharla. Brodie leapt forward, shoving the girl to the ground as the tail slammed into the wall, sending bricks and mortar flying.

Chad ducked and fired the gun again, this time aiming for the creature's body. He hit it, but bullet simply bounced off.

Sharla rolled and fired at the creature's eye, but missed and now the monster started towards them like a tank.

Brodie climbed to her feet, ran at the creature and jumped, her entire body weight hitting the center of the creature's eye. It screeched in pain, making a sound like torn metal as its tail whipped around catching her in the center of her back. She went flying.

'Run!' Sharla screamed.

Brodie was dazed, couldn't tell up from down. Then she felt Sharla grab her arm and drag her along the ground. Chad grabbed her other arm. They stumbled up the street, the monster screeching behind. They ran two more blocks, the pain in her back slowly subsiding.

It sounded like the monster was still following. They turned a corner—and Brodie's mouth fell open in amazement.

'How the hell —' she started.

'Keep moving!' Sharla commanded.

Somehow, at some time in the past, an ocean liner had ended up in the middle of the street. Brodie could not guess at how it happened. It appeared the ship had been picked up and dropped from a height. It had toppled over, reducing the buildings on one side to rubble.

They were at the bow. Sharla led them up a pile of rubble to a lower deck. Brodie could still hear the creature in pursuit, but it was far behind. It gave a final plaintive roar as Sharla dragged open a rusty door, pushed them inside and slammed it shut.

Sharla pulled out a flashlight, barely penetrating the murky gloom. She turned it on Chad. 'You idiot!' she hissed. 'Why did you fire the gun?'

'I'm sorry.' He looked genuinely apologetic. 'I fired it by accident.'

'Guns don't go off by themselves!'

'This one did!'

Sharla looked like she wanted to punch him in the face.

Brodie stepped between them. 'What's done is done,' she said. 'Now we need to keep moving.'

The other girl shot a final angry glance at Chad. 'One more mistake like that and you can both go it alone,' she said. 'You understand?'

Chad nodded. Sharla shone the flashlight down the tilted corridor. 'We'll go this way. It looks like it'll take us most of the way down the ship.'

They followed her. The ship appeared to have been in good condition when it was deposited here.

'How did this ship end up here?' Chad asked.

'How does anything happen?' Sharla

responded. 'James Price.'

'But why—'

'Who knows why that lunatic does anything? The sooner you kill him, the better.' She regarded them shrewdly. 'I don't suppose there's any spare room in that time machine. Is there?'

'You're looking for a ride?'

'Maybe.'

'I'm not sure taking you to the past would be such a good idea.'

'Why not?'

Chad thought. 'I'm no expert on this—'

'Obviously.'

'—but there's this whole thing about contaminating the time line.'

'Sounds like fun.'

'It's probably not. Suppose we took you to our time and something happened that stopped you from being born.' He paused. 'What would happen? Would you just disappear? Or would you continue to exist? But how could you because you had never been born?'

They were complicated questions and no-one had any answers to them. *Taking someone to the past is obviously a bad idea*, Brodie thought. *Who knows what you might break?*

Sharla might never be born. Most of the people they had encountered may never exist because their parents never met in the first place. Making changes in the past could cause irreparable harm.

Except, she reflected, it would seem the world would be a better place.

After all, it could hardly be any worse.

Could it?

'What's that sound?' Chad asked.

They stopped. At first Brodie could hear nothing, but then she heard squeaking. They turned, but there was only an empty corridor. Then Sharla angled the flashlight to the floor.

'A rat,' she said. 'And a big one too.'

It *was* large. Almost as big as a fully grown cat. Chad wondered if the yellow fog had affected it. Then he peered more closely.

'What's on its back?' he asked.

'They look like...' Brodie started. 'I don't know what they look like.'

In the next instant they had their answer as the rat ran towards them and launched itself into the air. Spreading a pair of leathery wings, it flew onto the wall, landed on the edge of a Van Gogh print and gave a high-pitched cry. Brodie snatched up a cup from the floor. She took careful aim and hit it. The creature swooped towards the ground and raced away.

'A rat with wings,' Brodie said. 'Now I've seen everything.'

'Not everything,' Sharla said. 'There are stranger things in the badlands.'

Brodie didn't want to think about them. Increasing their pace until they reached a set of swinging doors, they pushed through into the next section. After another minute, Chad heard a sound from behind. He glanced back and saw the double doors were wedged open.

That's strange, he thought. *We closed them. How—.*

'Sharla,' he said. 'Point your torch back down

139

the hall.'

She did. Dozens of rats were pushing into the hallway. The nearest was only a few feet away.

It launched into the air and flew directly at them.

Chapter Twenty-One

The creature flew at Chad. He stood frozen in shock as it headed directly towards his face. It was only at the last instant that Brodie's gloved fist struck out, swatting it away in mid-flight.

'Don't shoot at them!' Sharla shouted. 'It will just bring more.'

'Run!' Brodie yelled.

They ran, followed by a stampede of clawed feet. Chad wanted to use his powers against them. He could incinerate them in an instant, but he needed his suit intact. The next doors were still thirty feet away. He doubted they would reach them in time.

'To the left!' Brodie yelled. 'Go left!'

She disappeared through an open door with Sharla following. Chad was last. He leapt through the door just as a rat slammed into his back. He threw himself to the ground and rolled about, trying to dislodge it, screaming in panic. Normally he was in complete control, but that was when he had his powers. Now they amounted to nothing. He was helpless.

He saw Brodie aim a savage kick at the rat. It spun across the room, slammed into the far wall and lay still. Sharla had already bolted the door shut. One rat had been half-way through; its splattered remains stained the floor. A thumping sound came from the other side as its companions threw themselves against the door in desperation.

They were in a private cabin, lit by a single porthole. Sharla shone her torch around. Another door led to the bathroom, but this did not even contain a window.

'There's only one way out of here,' she said, pointing to the window. It was barely big enough for an infant let alone a teenager. Brodie examined it closely before peering about the cabin. She upended a bed, breaking off a six-foot metal strut.

'We might be able to solve this with a lever and some good old fashioned grunt,' she said, setting to work on the window.

Within minutes she had removed the casing. It took another half-an-hour to lever back enough of the bulkhead so that they could squeeze through. Now at the stern of the vessel, they were able to drop down a few feet onto the remains of a shattered building and continue their journey.

The remainder of the day passed without incident. After everything that had happened, Chad expected bizarre creatures to attack them from every corner, but the streets were surprisingly quiet. Only the fog remained, swirling and moving like a living thing. Chad saw the outside of his helmet was fogging up from the murky substance. He tried cleaning it, but only seemed to make it worse.

'Can someone help me out?' he asked.

Brodie cleaned it as he returned the favor.

'This would've been more fun if we were applying sun tan lotion on a sun drenched beach,' he said.

'You wish,' Brodie said, smiling. 'Let's stay focused.'

'We'll need to find a place to crash,' Sharla said. 'I know a building nearby.'

Her timing was good. By the time they arrived

at a brownstone a few streets away, the sky had turned a shade of murky brown; it was almost night. Sharla took them inside. An old spring mattress blocked the stairs. The girl pushed it aside and they climbed to a room on the second floor. It was surprisingly clean.

'I've stayed here a few times,' she explained. 'We should be fine just as long as we stay quiet.' She glared pointedly at Chad. 'No shooting.'

The night passed slowly. Chad found himself waking every few hours. It was impossible to sleep comfortably in the suits. He felt hot and sticky, as if he were sleeping inside a plastic bag. He was hungry too. They had eaten before leaving, but his stomach was rumbling loud enough to wake the dead.

He heard the others breathing through the comm system. Sharla's breathing was deep and rhythmical, Brodie's shallow and faster.

When he next opened his eyes he found Brodie shaking his shoulder.

'Come on, sleeping beauty,' she said. 'Time to move.'

They continued across the badlands, the fog dancing and tumbling around them. It was like being in an immense cave. Distance was impossible to gage because there was no horizon. The only evidence of open space was the ever constant sun, a brown disk in the sky.

By late morning Chad was starving. They hadn't eaten for almost a day and a half.

'Any chance of food?' he asked.

'Sure,' Sharla said. 'You find a way to squeeze food through the filter and you can eat all you want.'

Great, he thought. *Starvation will kill me if the gas doesn't.*

'We're almost there,' Sharla said an hour later. 'I can see the wall from here.'

Chad wasn't sure how she saw anything in this murky mess, but within minutes a dark shape appeared. He felt a sense of immense relief; somehow they had survived this nightmare landscape.

'Yay,' he croaked. 'Let's party.'

'There's a subway tunnel ahead,' Sharla said.

'It's a way into Manhattan.'

They had started to descend the stairs when the girl stopped.

'Damn,' she said. 'We've got a problem. I broke my torch back there and we'll need light to find the cross-tunnel.'

Chad thought for a moment. 'I can provide light,' he said. 'All we need.'

'But you can't use your powers without removing your suit,' Brodie pointed out.

'What if I just take my glove off?' he asked Sharla. 'Just for a few minutes.'

'There's less fog down here,' she said. 'You might end up with some skin irritation, but it wouldn't be permanent. Wait till we get further in though.'

They continued to the bottom. The murky light was sufficient to break though the gloom as they climbed over the barriers onto the concourse. Finally, Sharla said, 'Okay Chad,' she said, 'this is as far as we can get. We need light.'

He carefully unzipped the glove. Flexing his

hand, he immediately felt the strange fog twirling around his bare fingers.

'Okay,' he said. 'Let's make this quick.'

He created a small flame above his palm. It immediately illuminated their faces—and that of a man standing behind Brodie. The stranger wore no shirt. His skin stretched painfully over his rib. His eyes receded so far into his head that they were almost invisible. Below the sunken orbs, his cheeks were missing entirely, making his teeth look like rows of tiny tombstones.

Before Chad could utter a warning, the stranger leapt onto Brodie and bit her shoulder.

Chapter Twenty-Two

Brodie screamed.

Chad punched the man as hard as he could in the face. The stranger fell backwards and Chad followed up with a blast of fire. It struck him in the chest and he gave a single inarticulate cry before shuddering once and expiring on the spot. Creating a ring of fire, he illuminated the concourse. Empty. Chad examined Brodie's wound. The bite had pierced her suit; blood seeped from the injury.

'We have to get you out of here,' he said to Brodie. 'You need a tetanus shot and bandages.'

Sharla was staring at Brodie with a troubled expression. 'We're almost in Manhattan,' she said. 'Let's get moving.'

She led them down to a platform, onto the tracks and continued along a tunnel, reaching a blockage where the ceiling had collapsed. Sharla knew the way well. She led them over the rubble to a metal ladder someone had placed there years before. At the top of the hole was an abandoned apartment.

They stripped off their suits. Chad was relieved to be free of the sticky garments. He was a lather of sweat and he stunk of body odor. They all did. He examined Brodie's shoulder. It had already filled with pus. Exchanging glances with Sharla, he saw she was strangely silent, staring at Brodie without speaking.

'What?' Chad demanded. 'What aren't you saying?'

Sharla pursed her lips. 'I've seen people bitten before by those things...'

'And?'

'And they don't survive.'

'What?'

Brodie scrambled to her feet. 'That's ridiculous,' she said, laughing nervously. 'I feel fine.'

'Maybe your powers will fight off the infection,' Sharla said. 'But every other person has died.'

Chad asked, 'Is there a doctor around here?'

'A few blocks away.'

They abandoned the suits and Sharla took

them to a brownstone three blocks away. Sharla gave a coded knock at the door and it was eased open by an elderly woman with steel-grey hair.

'This is Robin,' Sharla said. 'She will do what she can for Brodie.'

'Are you leaving?' Chad asked.

'I have to get back to my own life,' she said, briefly hugging them. 'Good luck with your mission. I hope it goes well.'

The old woman invited them into a living room on the ground floor, offering them seats, but she was already staring at Brodie's shoulder.

'What happened to you?' she asked. 'Have you been bitten?'

They explained what had happened and the woman's face fell. 'Sharla should have explained to you,' she said. 'This is extremely serious.'

'She said no-one survived this sort of bite,' Chad said. The words sounded foreign to him even as he said them. It meant Brodie could die, but that was ridiculous. Brodie couldn't die. *She was Brodie*. He added, 'Brodie's been modified,' he said. 'She's got three times normal strength and speed. She'll be okay. Right?'

'Her powers will help,' Robin said, examining the wound. 'The people who live in the badlands have mutated. I'm not even sure they're still human. I'll clean and dress the wound and give you some antibiotics.'

Robin didn't say anything after that. She worked on Brodie's shoulder, wiping away the pus and stitching the bite marks closed. Finally, she gave Brodie some medication and told her to rest.

'We'll see how you are in a few hours,' she said.

'I feel sleepy,' Brodie said. 'Is that the pills?'

'Your body is fighting the infection,' Robin said, settling Brodie into a bed in the next room. Within seconds, she was asleep and Robin had returned to Chad. 'We'll monitor her condition,' she said.

'And if she worsens?'

'I've never seen anyone survive a bite from one of those creatures,' she said. 'I think you need to prepare yourself for the worst. Your friend might die.'

Your friend might die. The words rang in Chad's head. *Your friend might die.*

Exhausted, he settled into a chair as Robin left the room. He had hardly slept the previous night and barely eaten. Now he had to work out what to do about Brodie. If her condition worsened...

The next thing he knew, Robin was shaking his arm. He blinked, looking about in confusion. Somehow, he had fallen asleep, slumped in the chair. 'Brodie,' he said. 'Is she all right?'

'I'm afraid she's very unwell,' Robin said. 'You'd better come.'

He followed Robin to the surgery where Brodie now lay on a surgical bed with her shoulder bandaged. Her eyes were shut, but they eased open when Chad spoke her name.

'I'm very tired,' she said. 'Let me go back to sleep.'

Robin removed the bandage from her shoulder and Chad drew in his breath. The wound was severely inflamed. It had started to turn black. The cuts in her flesh had reopened and were seeping more pus.

The doctor drew Chad to one side. 'The antibiotics have not worked,' she said. 'She may only have a few hours.'

'That ridiculous!' he snapped. 'There must be something we can do!'

Robin thought. 'There *is* a Doctor by the name of Steven Bryce in Berkeley Heights,' she said. 'He has some powerful medicines, far stronger than anything I have.'

'What's the address?'

She gave him the details. The suburb lay several miles west of Manhattan. Robin gripped his arm. 'But you'll never get there in time,' she said. 'It's a full day's walk.'

Chad nodded. An idea was forming in his mind, but he didn't like it. He asked Robin about the air defenses over the city, but she just repeated what Old Axel had told them: fighter craft attacked unauthorized vessels.

'What are you thinking?' she asked him.

'I'm thinking about flying,' Chad said.

'Except I might end up killing us both.'

Chapter Twenty-Three

'You can fly?' Robin's face brightened immediately. 'That's fantastic. You might—'

'No,' he said, cutting her short. 'That's the problem. I can't fly. Not really.'

Doctor Michaels, a scientist at the Agency, had told him he could use his powers to fly. By creating a raft of superheated air, he could ride it through the sky like a surfboard. The scientist had offered to work with him, but the idea had terrified Chad.

Not that he would have admitted that fear to anyone. He was *The Chad* which meant he didn't show fear. They had been living in Las Vegas at the time and he had gone out into the desert to practice, eventually gaining proficiency at flying short distances. He had quickly found the flying to be the easy part—the landings were harder. More than once, he had misjudged the distance between himself and the ground and had crashed hard enough to bruise his body—and his pride.

So he had given up on the idea, driving it completely from his mind.

Until now.

Because now Brodie would die unless he flew her to this doctor.

He went onto the roof of Robin's house and stared at the sky. *It's always so easy for Axel*, he thought. *He flies as if he's got wings.* Chad had always felt like a tightrope walker. One wrong move and he would hurtle to the ground.

The memories were so terrifying he had even suffered nightmares, waking in the dead of night, dripping sweat. The one consolation as he lay in the dark was the knowledge he would never need to fly again.

He went downstairs to Robin's surgery. 'How long has she got?' he asked. 'To live, I mean.'

'A few hours,' Robin said. 'Maybe not that long.' She stared into his face. 'I can understand your fear.'

'I'm not afraid—' He stopped. 'No, I *am* afraid. I'm terrified. I might fall from the sky. I might drop Brodie by accident. Anything could happen.'

'You shouldn't do it then,' Robin said, gently. 'It sounds like your chances of succeeding are slim.'

'Slim?' He laughed bitterly. 'They're almost zero.'

Robin continued to speak, but Chad was staring at Brodie's face. No-one would ever know if he did nothing. No-one knew about his experiments in the desert. It would be a secret he could keep forever.

Except *he* would know and that was enough.

He had a second secret too, one he had hardly dared to acknowledge himself. He thought he was in love with Brodie. He wasn't sure, and it had never been a line of thinking he wanted to pursue. She was Axel's girlfriend, after all, and they loved each other and that was that.

But sometimes Chad wondered how life would be if she were not dating Axel. If she had *never* dated Axel, then everything would have been completely different. She might even have been with him from the very beginning.

He swallowed. No matter who she was dating, he would not let her die. Never. Picking her up, she stirred groggily in his arms. Dark rings had formed around her eyes. 'Are we at the beach?' she asked. 'I want to go swimming again.'

'No,' he said. 'You're not well. I'm taking you to a doctor.'

He carried her to the roof, his hands shaking, as a paralyzing fear gripped his chest. *This was crazy!* They would both get killed! But what sort of man would he be if he didn't try?

I'm The Chad! he thought. *I'm a superhero!*

Now he had to act like one.

Robin was at his elbow. 'Evolution gave us fear as an advantage,' she said. 'Run or fight. Changing your view of fear can change your feelings.'

'Thanks,' he grunted.

Chad formed a raft of heat with his mind. Robin stepped back as he made it superhot. Then he ran forward with Brodie in his arms and leapt onto it. For one horrifying moment he started to sink into it, but then he remembered the advice of Doctor Michaels.

You need to create a cushion of cold directly above the heated layer to protect yourself.

So he did this and the heat immediately subsided. He focused on projecting the raft forward and he started across the roof. Robin called out *good luck*, but he didn't reply. The raft headed over the edge of the roof and they started to drop.

For one terrifying second he thought he would plunge to the street below. Then he refocused again on the raft, making it more powerful, and it lifted him again. *Keep moving forward*, he told himself. *Onwards and upwards.* Within seconds he was high above Manhattan.

He was frightened—his whole body shook like a jellyfish—but he was alive. Sweat was dancing a jig down his back. His hair was plastered to his head. This was working. Somehow. His first goal was to aim for New Jersey. Some of its distinctive landmarks were visible in the distance. If everything went well, he might have Brodie at the doctor's within the hour.

Then he spotted something from the corner of his eye.

'Oh no,' he muttered.

A small, black dot was slicing across the horizon, growing larger by the second.

'I want to go to the beach,' Brodie said. 'I need to swim...'

Chad increased his speed and was soon speeding over the city buildings. Unfortunately the object in the sky had adjusted direction towards him and had increased velocity. It was a guided missile.

'Where's the beach?' Brodie murmured.

Chad felt his arms shaking worse than ever. He needed to land—and quickly—except he was too high up. Getting to the ground would take over a minute. And what if the missile followed them all the way down?

He had to go faster. He increased speed again, but the missile was still heading straight towards him. It was less than a mile away. Now only a thousand feet. He only had seconds to act so now he diverted his attention, creating a solid sheet of ice in mid air.

As long as the missile stuck it—

The missile slammed into the sheet and exploded. The forward impact from the shrapnel rained towards Chad and Brodie. He threw up a second ice shield to protect them.

Chad almost laughed out loud. *We're alive!* Not a single piece of the missile had hit them. He had never felt so elated in his life.

Then his flying raft evaporated and they began falling earthward.

Chapter Twenty-Four

Night had fallen across the island. Dan sat huddled in the *Liber8tor* galley nursing a cup of hot chocolate. He had returned to the ship after Henry had gone missing. He did not believe the boy was in immediate danger. He had, after all, survived on the island for some time; he must know a hundred hiding places. Dan was more concerned about himself and the ship.

'Have you picked up any life forms?' he asked Ferdy.

'The *Liber8tor* senses have not,' Ferdy said. 'It would seem that whatever you heard in the jungle does not show up on our senses.'

Great, Dan thought. *Just what I needed.*

'Are the weapons systems working?' he asked.

'They are operating at normal levels.'

'So we have missiles...'

'Missiles and laser systems,' Ferdy said. 'However, there is nothing specifically designed for monsters.'

'Are you saying you don't believe me?'

'It does seem strange that the *Liber8tor* sensors cannot pick up the creature.'

'The sensors couldn't pick up Henry either.'

'That is true.'

Dan wondered where Henry had gone. Probably back to his cell in the laboratory complex. 'Were you able to find out anything more about the Japanese during the war?' he asked.

'Ferdy has an enormous amount of information about Japan during the war. The Japanese attacked Pearl Harbor on December seventh—'

'No, I mean the Japanese on his island.'

'Unfortunately not.'

Dan finished his drink and went to his room. The chamber was designed to house four Tagaar warriors, but Dan had converted it into a home away from home. The other bunks had been stripped, now holding televisions and gaming equipment. He considered playing *Zombie Attack Squad*, but decided he didn't feel like it. The last thing he needed was a reminder about monsters and the living dead.

He read for a while before turning in. Another light remained on in the corridor all night. Chad always teased him by calling it his nightlight, although they all found the crew quarters claustrophobic as there were few windows around the ship.

Closing his eyes, he doubted he would sleep at all, but found himself opening them again several hours later. He wondered what had awakened him. Usually he slept all night. Maybe the others were back.

'Axel?' he called. 'Hey guys.'

There was silence, but a shadow moved across the hall. He went to the door.

'Brodie?' The hall was empty. 'Who's there?'

No answer.

'Ferdy?'

Ferdy's voice came back immediately. 'Yes, friend Dan.'

'Is anyone else aboard *Liber8tor*?'

'The only ones aboard *Liber8tor* are Ferdy

164

and Dan.'

'Are you sure?'

'Nothing is certain, Dan. It is possible that an inter-dimensional singularity has opened up, allowing an alien from another dimension to invade the ship.'

'Uh, how likely is that?'

'One chance in several hundred billion.'

'I think we can rule that out.'

A sound came from the galley. Dan asked Ferdy to turn on all the lights both inside and outside *Liber8tor*. A metal pipe lay in his bedroom. Retrieving it, he crept down the hall. An elevator and metal ladder led up. Dan chose the ladder, but used his mind to send the metal pipe up first. Nothing attacked it, so it carefully climbed to the top, peering about. He saw the table, storage compartments, freezer, ovens and benches—but no-one else.

'Henry?' he called. 'Are you here?'

Silence.

Then Ferdy's voice came from the loud speaker system. 'There is no-one else on board the ship, friend Dan.'

'You also said there were no monsters on the island!'

'The *Liber8tor* sensors—'

'Screw the *Liber8tor* sensors!' Dan snapped. The tension was really getting to him. 'I'm sorry. I didn't mean to be rude.'

'That's all right, friend Dan. Fear is a difficult emotion.'

'Do you...I mean, do you still feel fear now that you're...'

'Now that Ferdy's consciousness is contained within the *Liber8tor* computers? Yes. It is an irrational feeling, but it doesn't make it any less real.'

'Uh...which means?'

'Ferdy understands how you're feeling.'

'Thanks.' Dan felt a little better. He poured himself a glass of water and sat it on the bench. From the freezer, he pulled out a selection of freeze-dried packets that all looked like they belonged in a lab.

'We've got K'tresh and B'klah and Gar'kah,' he said, reading the labels. 'Ferdy, can't we just order out for pizza?'

'The nearest pizza shop is several thousand miles away.'

'Really? There's not one on the island?'

'If Dan is making a joke—'

The room went dark: the lights, the computers, even the emergency signs above the doors. Dan found himself in pitch black darkness. It was like being inside a cave, a deep cavern miles beneath the ground, and without a light. Dan dropped the food packets. They made a clattering sound and he almost jumped a mile. He had laid the pipe down when he first entered. Now he tried bringing it to him, but couldn't do it without seeing it first.

His heart pounding, Dan slowly made his way around the bench. Where had he sat the pipe? *It's here somewhere.* His hands slid over the cold tabletop. *Where is it?*

Clink.

Dan's heart exploded in his chest. Something was on the other side of the table! Something alive! He could hear it breathing!

Where was the pipe? Where had he—?

The lights snapped back on and Dan stared in absolute horror—at nothing. He was alone in the galley. No monster. All was exactly as it was before the lights went out.

'—then it is a funny joke,' Ferdy finished.

'Ferdy,' Dan said in a strangled voice, 'what made the power fail?'

'The power has not failed.'

'Everything went off! You stopped speaking and I was standing here in the dark!'

'Ferdy has no recollection of those events. The third king of England was—'

'I don't care if he was the third king of Pluto!' Dan yelled. 'The power failed!'

'There is no record of the power failing.'

'Check the *Libr8tor* sensors! Double-check them. I was here alone, but then something else was in here too!'

'If you are referencing the Schrodinger's Cat hypothesis—'

'Forget Shoddy Ring's Cat! Just check the sensors!' Dan tried to calm himself. 'Has anything entered the ship in the last few minutes?'

'There is no record of anything entering or leaving the ship,' Ferdy said.

But Dan had stopped listening to him because now he was staring at his glass of water on the table. Now he understood the sound in the darkness, the *clink* that had set his hair on end.

The glass had been turned upside down.

And it was still filled with water.

Chapter Twenty-Five

A strange calm overcame Chad as he fell. Perhaps facing imminent death focused his mind; he had to instantly form another raft of heat beneath him and it had to do it *now*. He created the raft—a massive surge of heat exploded under him—and then built the cold platform over it.

Their descent slowed but did not stop. They fell past a skyscraper. Chad knew they were lucky; they would have slammed into it if they had been directly over the building. He focused on making the raft of air hotter. And hotter.

They slowly ground to a halt. Chad looked across at another building. Many of the windows were broken, but on this level he saw a rough looking woman staring out at him in amazement. He forced a smile and focused on ascending.

Reaching the top of the building, Chad angled them towards the roof. He still couldn't work out how to land, so he shielded Brodie's body with his own as they plowed into the roof where he lay, shaking uncontrollably. He couldn't go on. He was shaking so hard he couldn't even stand.

Someone muttered his name.

'Chad...Chad...where are you?'

'Brodie?'

She was half draped over him. He gently laid her on the roof. 'How are you feeling?' he asked.

'Not well.'

He examined her shoulder. It was charcoal colored, and looked terrible with dark green pus flowing from the wound.

'I feel so weak,' Brodie said, her eyes unfocused. 'I can't move...'

'You're going to be okay,' he said. 'We're both going to be okay.'

Chad lifted her up again with a renewed determination. He had stopped shaking now. Brodie wouldn't last much longer. He would get her to a doctor or die trying.

He created another raft, lifted Brodie and he leapt onto it. This time it was easier and he felt a sense of renewed confidence.

'Let's go,' he said.

The raft carried him away from the building. He concentrated on pouring the speed on and this time he zoomed across the city with the wind tearing at his hair. He glanced around to see if another missile had been fired, but the sky was clear.

He was lower than he had been on his first flight. *Maybe the missiles are only activated when they detect movement at a certain height.* He hoped he was right. Increasing speed again, he passed New Jersey and Plainfield.

Looking behind him, he saw a clear blue sky—except for three tiny dots on the horizon.

Not again!

He went faster, glancing back occasionally. The dots were larger now and they looked different to the missile. He spotted a building among others that was still in one piece.

Now for the hard part, he thought. *Landing.*

He slowed and within seconds was directly over the roof. He gently lowered himself, but instead of coming in at an angle, he decreased the heat of the raft beneath him.

Slowly, slowly, slowly...

Touchdown.

Chad was so thrilled he wanted to burst into song. He checked Brodie. She was breathing, but unconscious. A distant sound cut the air. The three shapes weren't missiles, they were those rotor ships he and Brodie had encountered at Times Square.

He found a set of stairs leading down. A line of glass blocks ran down one wall; they must have looked quite fashionable once. Now they were covered in green mold. Through them he was able to make out the rotor craft, flying tight circles over the area.

Someone cleared their throat. Chad looked around to see a teenage boy peering up the stairs at him.

'Are you the flying person?' he asked.

'Uh, yes.'

'Come with me.'

The boy started down. Chad followed him. This kid might know where to find Doctor Bryce.

'We know about you,' the boy said. 'My name's Joshua. The Manhattan faction was able to get a message through.'

Bless you Robin, Chad thought. She must have sent news of his mission.

Chad followed the boy to the front door. The droning of the rotor craft continued for a few more minutes before they disappeared behind distant buildings. Joshua led Chad to a residential house a few blocks away. Entering through the rear, Chad found himself in a neat kitchen.

A man appeared. He had a long white beard, but his hair was thinning on top. His clear blue eyes examined Chad.

'You're the time traveling boy,' he said.

'We need your help,' Chad said. Brodie weighted a ton. 'She was bitten by—'

'I know. Bring her through.'

Minutes later Brodie was on a hospital gurney in a makeshift surgery. Modern medical equipment had been installed in the art deco home, looking strangely out of place. The doctor gripped his shoulder.

'Sit down, son,' he said. 'Get some rest.'

Chad didn't argue. He felt exhausted. The doctor gave him some tinned meat and he devoured this, but he had not slept properly for days. His legs were so shaky he was ready to collapse. By the time Chad finished eating, his eyes were closing. He lay back on a lounge.

The sun was low in the sky when he woke. It was almost dark. Joshua was gone and the rest of the house was silent. A chill went through him. Was Brodie safe? Maybe this whole thing was a setup. Maybe he'd walked into an Agency trap.

Footsteps approached, the door from the hallway eased open and a head peered through the gap.

'Brodie!' he yelled.

'Hey Chad.' She peered at him shyly.

Chad ran to her. He gave her a hug and pulled back to stare at her. Her hair was a mess, her eyes were puffy and she looked pale and drawn. But she had never looked more beautiful.

So he kissed her.

Chapter Twenty-Six

The next morning, Dan asked Ferdy to run a complete check of the ship's sensors while he checked the *Liber8tor*'s external doors. They were firmly locked from the inside. Nothing could have entered the ship—and yet it did.

'The ship's sensors show nothing out of the ordinary—' Ferdy reported.

'Great.'

'—but Ferdy *has* been able to find evidence of a power loss to the ship.'

'So I wasn't imagining it,' Dan said.

'Correct.'

I knew I wasn't crazy, Dan thought. *Something was on board the ship and the same something turned the glass over without spilling a drop.*

'Ferdy,' he said. 'I'm going back to where I found Henry. I think he may have hidden there overnight.'

'Do you think that's wise? What if there really is a creature roaming about on the island?'

'There *is* a creature,' Dan told him. 'And we need to keep Henry safe from it.'

He packed a bag with food and water. He also put in some metal bars from a *Liber8tor* storage locker. They might be valuable weapons if he encountered the monster, assuming he was able to fight a creature that was able to move through locked doors.

Cutting through the jungle, Dan returned to the buildings he had found the previous day. Climbing down to the lab, he picked up some papers from a bench and stuffed them into the backpack. They were in Japanese, but Ferdy could translate them. Then he cautiously started back to the cell, passing the moldy growth on the wall. The smell was so bad it was almost gut-churning. *How could Henry stand to be down here?*

'Henry?' he called. 'Are you there?'

The cell was empty.

Damn, he thought. This would be more difficult than he expected.

He called out the boy's name again as he

scrambled up the incline to the jungle above. Once again he was greeted by silence. He navigated through the dense jungle, reaching the boat he had explored the previous day. He searched for footprints, but found none.

Where had Henry gone?

Dan continued along the beach, angling inland towards *Liber8tor*. He asked Ferdy if there were any other buildings on the island. Ferdy told him no. 'However,' he continued, 'Ferdy has been able to identify some caves near the mountain. They could be used as a shelter.'

Dan thought. Caves were not so different to the underground cell in which he had first found Henry. Maybe he used them for shelter too.

'I'll check them out,' Dan said. 'In the meantime, can you examine these documents and see what you can find on the net?'

Dan took pictures of them so Ferdy could scan them into the ship's computer, and left for the cave. It took some time to find. The entrance was a thin crevice caused by rock fall, nestled between some trees on the mountain's east side. Dan peered in the opening.

'Hello!' he called. 'Henry! Are you in there?'

His voice rebounded about the interior of the cave. Then he heard, 'Dan? Is that you?'

'Henry!'

Snapping on the flashlight, Dan entered. It was dry and dusty inside with three separate tunnels leading away. Dan checked for footprints in the fine dust, but he could see none.

'Dan?'

The voice came from the middle tunnel. Dan followed it downhill. After a minute the ground flattened out and he found himself faced with a choice of two passages. He called Henry's name again, and received an answering cry from his left.

It was here that he found a shape huddled alone in the darkness. Henry had pushed himself into a recess in the wall, the book still firmly clenched in his hand. He leapt out, throwing his arms around Dan.

'I come here sometimes to hide from the monster,' he explained, dry tears on his cheeks. 'This time I got lost and couldn't find my way out.'

'It's daylight,' Dan said. 'The monster is gone.'

'I heard the monster.'

'What?' Alarm bells rang in Dan's mind.

'It's here in the tunnels.'

'When did you hear it?'

A low growl came from the tunnel behind. He spun about, waving the torch. The shadows danced and weaved in the recesses of the walls.

Then he saw it, a figure darted across the tunnel. Dan tipped the metal bars onto the ground, his heart in his throat. He was scared, but not so scared that he couldn't fight. He grabbed Henry, pushing the small boy behind him.

'Is there another way out of here?' he asked.

'I'm not sure,' the boy sobbed. 'I got lost—'

Dan felt a breeze across the back of his neck. 'There's a way out behind us,' he said. 'Hold my hand.'

He gave the small boy's hand a reassuring squeeze and led him along the tunnel. The ground ahead of them was rough underfoot and led upwards. He used his powers to levitate a metal bar behind them as another growl reverberated around the tunnel.

His torch illuminated a dark shape fifty feet behind. Focusing on the bar, he fired it with all his might down the middle of the tunnel. It slammed into the shadowy form and the figure screamed and staggered. It fell to one side. The shape was double his height, humanoid shaped. Dan could make out little more. At least the creature was not impervious to attack.

Keeping Henry behind him, Dan continued to slowly retreat up the tunnel. The monster came after them and Dan launched another bar at it.

The monster screamed again as if impaled. It collapsed against the wall. Holding Henry's hand, Dan turned and dragged the boy down the tunnel until he spotted a faint glow. It came from the first chamber Dan had entered, where the three tunnels branched from.

We're out, he thought. *We've made it.*

Then the shape appeared in the doorway of the

middle tunnel.

'Run, Henry!' Dan screamed. 'Run!'

The boy sped past him as Dan produced another pipe from his backpack. A smell hit him, a strange stench of decay. Then the dark shape leapt towards him and he fired the metal bar into its chest. The monster cried out again and flung out an arm, knocking Dan backwards. He hit the wall, fell and blindly staggered into warm sunlight.

He turned to face the creature.

Alone.

Chapter Twenty-Seven

'I'm Marcus, the leader of the South-Eastern resistance,' the man explained. 'It's my job to keep you alive.'

Chad and Brodie were sitting in a home a block away from the doctor's house. They had been relocated here after Brodie's rapid recovery. Chad was still amazed she had healed so quickly, but he knew there were many amazing things about her.

Like she was a good kisser.

Until she pushed him away.

'I'm going out with Axel,' she said. 'You can't do things like that.'

Chad had mumbled an apology, flushed with embarrassment and they had not spoken about the incident since.

Still, Chad could not forget the taste of Brodie's lips against his mouth. Despite everything she'd been through, her illness and not washing for days, despite all that, she still tasted of spring.

Glorious spring.

'There's some people who wants to meet you,' Marcus continued. 'Some governors.'

'Governors? What are they?'

'Resistance leaders. You don't know them, but they know you.'

'Great,' Chad said. 'Some unknown hotshots want to meet us. What do they want? An autograph?'

'I'd appreciate some respect,' Marcus said, his eyes narrowing. 'We're risking our lives just to help you.'

Chad apologized. 'We appreciate everything you've done for us,' he said, 'but we need to find our friends.'

'That'll happen. Eventually. But you need to understand that a lot of people want you dead. We need to keep you safe.'

'We know we're not popular with the Agency.'

'It's not just the Agency,' Marcus said. 'People have heard you want to change history. Not everyone's happy about that.'

'Why not?' Brodie asked in surprise.

'People have families. Wives. Children. Have you thought about how this will change history? Anyway, we're taking you to the rendezvous point to meet the governors.'

Chad sighed. It seemed like a long way round to find Axel and Ebony. Marcus took them to an underground subway tunnel where a makeshift vehicle, a cross between an automobile and a railway handcar, sat on the tracks. Two seats from a sedan faced each other on the handcar, with a petrol engine underneath, and driver's chairs and control columns at both ends.

'That's innovative,' Brodie said.

'The height of human technology,' Marcus said grimly. 'I won't be joining you for this part of the journey. But I wish you luck, whatever happens.'

A man, appearing from the shadows, was introduced as Sketch. He was tall, thin and unshaven. His hair looked like it had not been washed in months and most of his teeth were missing.

Brodie greeted him cordially, but he merely grunted in reply. When she asked how long the journey would take, he told them six hours. That was the end of the conversation. Marcus bade them farewell and they climbed aboard the odd looking device. The man started the engine. It coughed a few times before roaring into life. Brodie and Chad sat next to each other, but Brodie was careful not to sit too close. She didn't want a repeat of the previous day.

The vehicle started slowly, but picked up speed. Within minutes it was roaring down the pitch black tunnel at top speed. The wind tore at Brodie's face and she closed her eyes. She wished there were lights. It was horrible moving through the dark without any reference to up or down.

Brodie allowed her mind to wander. Chad had saved her life; of that she had no doubt. She could dimly remember the immense pain in her body, the delirium and her flight across the city. She would be forever grateful he risked his life to save her.

She could also not forget the feel of Chad's mouth upon her own. It was not...unpleasant.

But she was Axel's girlfriend. Not that he

always acted like it. He seemed so much in his own head that he sometimes went for days without showing her any real affection. An uncomfortable thought had been lurking in the back of her mind for weeks. He said he loved her, but he didn't always show it. In fact, he hardly *ever* showed it.

Maybe they weren't meant to be together.

She had never acknowledged the idea before, and now it carved a deep emptiness inside her. Everything had happened so fast over the last few months; they had woken without their memories, become superheroes overnight and just as quickly become criminals on the run from the Agency.

Maybe she was never meant to be Axel's girlfriend.

But that didn't mean she was supposed to be with Chad.

Did it?

Squeezing her eyes tightly, she bowed her head as the vehicle moved through the darkness into a night that seemed to have no end.

Chapter Twenty-Eight

The monster was gone.

Dan stood at the entrance to the cave, his heart pounding, another pipe hovering in the air, but nothing attacked. He could not even hear the creature anymore. Dust swam about in the shaft of sunlight illuminating the interior. Beyond, there was nothing to see, as if the creature had disappeared into thin air.

Hot and disoriented, he stumbled backwards down the hill. He called Henry's name, but had no response. The boy had escaped into the jungle. He searched for him for another hour without success before heading back to *Liber8tor*.

'Ferdy,' he said, arriving back on *Liber8tor*'s bridge. 'I need information.'

'Certainly, friend Dan. The numerical value of pi is three point one four one five nine—'

It sounded like Ferdy could go on forever. 'Thanks, Ferdy. Not that sort of information. I need to know what you found out about those pages.'

'Ferdy discovered some very interesting

189

information.'

Silence.

'Do you want to share it?' Dan asked.

'Certainly,' Ferdy continued. 'The island *was* occupied by the Japanese during the war. A research laboratory was established, housing some of their most important biological scientists.'

'What were they researching?'

'The documents do not go into any details, but it is interesting that one scientist was Doctor Hiroto Satou. Prior to the start of World War Two, he was dismissed from two universities for his work in hybrid plant/animal research.'

'What does that mean? Exactly?'

'It seems he was trying to combine both plants and animals into a single organism.'

'Great,' Dan groaned. 'I'm fighting a plant...person...thing.'

'Dan?'

Dan explained his battle with the creature in the cave.

'Dan is risking his life unnecessarily,' Ferdy

said. 'You should wait until our friends return from their mission.'

'I'm old enough to deal with this myself.'

'It is not a reflection on your age. It is a well known adage that there is safety in numbers. Numerical superiority has long been a determining factor in winning battles.'

'I can't just hide here in the ship,' Dan said. 'Henry is out there alone.'

'Ferdy and Dan can search for your friend together. Liberator can carry out a grid search of the island.'

'I thought you were worried we might be picked up by Agency aircraft.'

'A low level sweep should be undetectable by Agency sensors.'

Dan nodded thoughtfully. He had wanted to handle this situation himself, showing he was as capable as everyone else. Just because he was small didn't mean he should be treated like a baby.

But the most important thing was keeping Henry safe. He had no idea how Henry had survived this long. Maybe the creature had been largely dormant until *Liber8tor* arrived on the island. Their arrival may have stirred it into action.

'Let's do it,' Dan said.

He took the helm and did the pre-check of their systems. Everything was normal. Firing up the engines, he brought them to full power, feeling the gentle surge of the engines as the ship lifted from the ground. He felt instantly better. He had have only been flying *Liber8tor* for a month, but it already felt like another appendage.

'How high can we fly?'

'A maximum of one hundred feet should be safe.'

Dan applied more acceleration. A whine radiated from the ship.

'Ferdy? What's that sound?'

'Thrust is being applied to the engines, but *Liber8tor* is not ascending.'

'Is there something wrong with the engines?'

'They are operating within normal parameters.'

'So what's wrong?'

'The ship appears to be tethered to the island.'

'By what?'

'Ferdy is unsure.'

Keeping his eye on the altimeter, Dan increased power. The ship was ten feet off the ground and rising. The whine in the engines increased as the ship started shuddering.

'What's happening, Ferdy?'

'Something is holding us back,' Ferdy said. 'It is trying to stop us from leaving.'

The *something* could only be one thing. The creature. Dan increased power to the thrusters again. He activated the exterior cameras and saw sand and plants flying away from the ship as the thrusters blasted the ground beneath them. Whatever was tying them to the island was nowhere to be seen. The ship rocked ominously from side to side.

'Heat is building in the engine manifold,' Ferdy said.

'What does that mean?'

'The close proximity of the firing thrusters to

the ground is creating a buildup of heat around the engines.'

The ship dipped wildly to one side and Dan was almost thrown to the floor. Clinging on for dear life, he tried to keep the ship level, but now it was tilting in the other direction. Something slammed into the ship. 'Ferdy! What was that?'

'Ferdy does not know.'

It hit the ship again.

'Is it the engines?'

'It is not the engines.'

The ship was almost sideways again. Dan had never flown the ship at this angle before. He wasn't sure what to do. The monster might tear the vessel apart if he landed, but he might tear it apart if he tried to take off.

'The engines are at sixty percent,' Ferdy reported. 'Seventy percent. Eighty percent -.'

'Load the aft torpedoes!'

'Loaded. But Ferdy must warn you that you may destroy the ship if you fire them.'

'What?'

'The resulting explosion would be too close to the engine housing. An explosion of that magnitude might cause it to rupture, resulting in the ignition of the fuel cells and the destruction of *Liber8tor*.'

Dan swore. *What was he going to do?*

'Hold on!' he yelled, although he doubted Ferdy actually had anything to hold on to. 'I'm going to try something.'

He decelerated, watching their altitude drop. For all the energy he had poured into the engines, he had reached a height of only twenty feet. Now they dropped to fifteen. And ten.

'How are the engine manifold...things?' Dan asked.

'They are at thirty percent. Twenty percent.'

'Good. Get ready.'

'For what?'

Dan didn't answer. Swallowing hard, he waited a few more seconds, continuing to descend as if he was about to land—and then he pushed the engines to full power. He was thrown back in his seat as the Libr8tor shot upwards. As if on a rope, it stopped and he was almost thrown from his seat. *A technologically advanced civilization,* Dan thought, *and they couldn't invent seat belts!* An ear piercing shriek came from the engines. Dan tried adjusting their direction and the ship tipped over.

Then they were free. Whatever had held them here released its grip as if the rope had broken. The ship surged forward. *Yes!* Dan shifted the control column. Now he just needed to bring the ship around.

But he was too late. The ship slammed sideways into the jungle. He decelerated as he fought to pull *Liber8tor* into a vertical position, but there was no time. The vessel rolled and suddenly Dan was thrown from his seat. He was on the ceiling. Then on a wall. He heard the sound of smashing as everything not secured below decks—personal belongings, kitchen utensils, tools, weaponry—was thrown upside down.

A command console exploded. The ship rolled one more time before it tumbled to a stop. The lights flickered on and off as Dan found himself lying on the floor. He had hit his head in the crash and blood oozed down one side of his face.

'Ferdy,' he groaned. 'What's the condition of the ship?' No answer. 'Ferdy?'

A hopeless sob burst from Dan as he understood the enormity of what he had done. He had destroyed the ship. He may have even killed Ferdy...

Chapter Twenty-Nine

The journey on the petrol driven handcar seemed to take forever. Finally Brodie became aware of it slowing. Opening her eyes, she saw a dim light in the distance that became an old subway platform, manned by people with guns. They did not move as Chad and Brodie, stiff and sore from their journey, gingerly disembarked.

The leader of the group introduced himself as Lightfoot. 'We'll be taking you to see the governors.'

'Just so long as we don't have to travel in the dark,' Chad said.

A man produced two black hoods and pairs of handcuffs.

'You've got to be kidding,' Brodie said.

'This is how we stay alive,' Lightfoot explained. 'If you get captured and tortured by the Agency, you can't reveal the location of HQ.'

'We're mods,' Chad told him. 'We could break through those cuffs in an instant.'

'Good for you.'

'We could just fight our way out of here if we wanted—'

'Chad,' Brodie said quietly.

Lightfoot glared at him. 'I'm just as happy if you turn around and walk back to New York,' he said. 'It makes no difference to me.'

'We've come this far,' Brodie said, shutting Chad down with a glance. 'We'll do as you say.'

The hoods were placed over their heads and Brodie again found herself in darkness. They climbed a set of stairs and a few minutes later were loaded into a van. The engine roared to life.

Brodie closed her eyes, but she had already slept on the railcar. She tried making conversation, but her captors gave her monosyllabic responses so she stayed quiet after that. The vehicle pulled onto a different kind of road, a dirt track. She lurched against Chad and once again felt an uncomfortable sensation in her stomach.

The van stopped. She heard men speaking. Some time later, the back opened and she was helped out. Her legs felt shaky as she tried to walk.

'Can you take the hoods off?' she heard Chad ask. 'And handcuffs?'

'Not yet,' a girl replied. 'In a minute.'

Brodie was led along a dirt path, up a few timber steps and into a building. She was put into a chair, and the hood and handcuffs were removed. Blinking, she wiped her eyes. They were in an old cabin. Through the window she saw distant trees and hills. It was late in the day. Chad looked fine. Then she turned to the girl who, presumably, had led them inside. She was slim with straight, red hair, and a pretty face, though with a scar across her chin.

The girl looked surprised. 'Who the hell *are* you?' she asked.

'We might ask you the same question,' Chad said. 'I'm really sick of all this cloak and dagger crap.'

'What are your names?'

Brodie told her.

The girl paled. 'Wait here,' she said. 'Don't move.' After she left, Brodie and Chad exchanged glances.

'This gets weirder and weirder,' Chad said.

'I know what you mean. That girl looked freaked when she saw us.'

'There's something else too. We need to talk.'

'About what?'

'You know.'

The kiss.

'I'm sorry I did that,' Chad said. 'But I'm not sorry it happened.'

'You have to put it out of your mind,' Brodie said, her heart beating faster. 'Axel's my boyfriend. I'm in love with him.'

'Are you sure?'

'Yes, I'm sure,' she said, although she wasn't. 'I'm your friend. That's all.'

'I would never want to break you guys up.' Chad swore. 'Axel's like a brother to me. I'd lay down my life for him, but that doesn't change how I feel.'

'I can't help how you feel.'

'So you're saying your feelings could never change?'

'Never.' She said the words firmly, but she knew she was being stupid. Never was a long time. As long as forever. 'I'm your friend and that's all I'll ever be.'

There was the scrape of feet on the floorboards outside. The door opened and the red-headed girl appeared.

'Here they are,' she said. 'Just like I told you.'

Two people entered after her. One was a woman with long red hair that had started to turn gray. The man was tall and strong, blonde and grim looking. Still, they recognized them immediately.

Brodie felt faint. 'You're us,' she said. 'Our older selves.'

She felt as if an electric current were running through her body. Now she knew how Axel felt when his older self had turned up. She stared into a face she knew well, but made older by the trials of time and life. But her eyes were the same. It was like looking through a telescope at herself.

'I don't know what this is about,' Old Brodie said, 'but it isn't going to work.'

'This is no scam,' Brodie said. 'We're from the past. And you're...' Her voice trailed off as she looked at Chad's older self. He had grown into a strong, powerful man, his boyish looks replaced by a rugged countenance. But she felt he had more than aged. He had become himself, into the man he was always supposed to be.

Chad was saying something. '...as much a surprise for us as it is for you,' he said. 'But this isn't some plot hatched up by the Agency. We're us, uh, you, but from the past.'

'Prove it,' Old Chad said.

It took almost half an hour for Chad and Brodie to explain how they had ended up there. It took just as long to convince Old Brodie they were telling the truth, but the older version of Chad wouldn't give in.

'It all sounds like an Agency plot to me,' he said.

'Are you always this much of a jerk?' Chad asked. 'I grow up to become some sort of douche bag?'

'Okay,' Old Chad nodded. 'Now I'm convinced. Only I could be *that* painful.'

'We've got to find Axel and Ebony, and return to our time,' Brodie said.

'That's easier said than done.'

'Why?'

Their older selves exchanged glances. 'It's a long story,' Old Chad said. 'We had a falling out and things have never been the same since.'

'So you know where he is?'

'We can contact him,' Old Brodie said, sighing. 'But we haven't spoken for years.'

Old Chad tapped a communicator badge on his chest.

'We're coming out,' he said. 'Turn off the VRG.'

'The VRG?' Chad said.

The scenery of hills and fields went dark. Old Brodie opened the door and motioned them outside. Instead of open sky, they saw a black ceiling. Blank walls surrounded them. Even the outside of the cabin appeared unfinished, like scenery on a movie set.

'This is the VRG,' Old Chad said. 'Virtual Reality Generator.'

'None of this is real?' Brodie asked.

'We're fifty feet underground,' Old Brodie said. 'There are probably places like this left on Earth, but this isn't one of them.'

'One thing's real,' Old Chad said. 'This is Tanya.' He studied their faces for a moment before continuing. 'She's our daughter.'

Chapter Thirty

We were fine until we entered the atmosphere.

Traveling in silence, I was thinking about the space station and all the people who had died so we could retrieve the temporal resonators. I knew it was necessary, but I couldn't help thinking they had families waiting for them. Families that would never see them again.

I tried to drive the horror of it away. *This is a brutal time.* I could understand why Old Axel wanted James Price dead. All this could be avoided by killing one person. Was one life too much to pay for peace?

'I'm getting some blips on radar,' Old Axel said. 'Some Agency ships are closing in on us.' He swore. 'I knew this was too easy.'

I shot a glance at Ebony.

Too easy. Sure.

Accelerating, he brought us in over North America, but it was obvious we weren't going to make it back to the East Coast. Old Axel took us into a sharp dive, heading into the heart of the country; the enormous storm that dominated the mid-west. Old Axel had referred to it earlier as The Eye. The closer we went, the more it resembled one. What would have been the white of the eye—the sclera—was relatively calm, but The Eye's cornea churned with swirling yellow fog that bubbled and frothed like a whirlpool.

Perhaps the most frightening part was the The Eye's iris. Like a human iris, it was black. Dead black. Nothing within it moved at all. I dreaded to think what—if anything—existed in that terrible darkness. If anything *could* exist in it.

The storm was like the shifting layer of a cake. At our altitude we could still see clear sky, with Agency ships on the horizon like a school of silver fish. Below us lay the biggest storm in history.

'There are twelve Agency ships closing in on us,' he said. 'Any second—' The ship jolted. 'They're firing.'

'I can deal with them,' I said. Taking on twelve Agency ships wouldn't be easy, but it wasn't impossible either. 'Open the rear hatch.'

'No.' The ship shuddered again. 'I can't afford for us to get separated.'

We were east of The Eye's cornea; Illinois or Missouri, in our time. Descending, the fog swallowed us as effectively as if we had been eaten by a monster. Nicotine colored clouds rushed by us as we dropped. Old Axel watched his controls intently, flying by instruments only.

He slowed the vessel and I began to make out shapes in the fog. A skyscraper. A bridge. We cruised low over the ground as the fog rushed by. Finally he landed the vessel with barely a bump. He was the best pilot I had ever seen.

We looked out at the storm. The freakish yellow wind may as well have been a curtain. It was impossible to see anything man-made or otherwise. We may have been in a desert, but I really had no idea.

'They won't follow us into the fog,' Old Axel said. 'Sensors don't work in the fog. Nothing works.'

'This storm—' Ebony started.

'It's not a storm,' he said. 'Because storms

don't last forever. It's a permanent fixture thanks to James Price. We're lucky it hasn't destroyed the planet.'

'What do we do?'

'We wait it out.' An explosion sounded somewhere off to our left. Old Axel swore. 'They're bombing the surface. Probably hoping to make a lucky hit.'

'What if a bomb hits us?' Ebony asked.

He looked worried. 'They're using dense particle charges. A direct hit would rupture the hull. It might even destroy the ship.' Another explosion shook the vessel. It seemed to come from right in front of us. 'We should sit tight.'

'You can't just use the fog as cover and fly us out of here?'

'The engines wouldn't take the constant battering.'

'Maybe I should just fly up there and—' I began.

'And take on a dozen ships? Don't be insane.' He went to the rear and produced three suits. Yellow in color, they looked like the sort of gear a decontamination worker would wear. 'Put these on. They'll protect you from the fog in case the hull is breached.'

'How long will we wait?' I asked.

'It could be a few days,' Old Axel said. 'I've been through this once before. We were stuck here a week.'

'A week?' Ebony said. 'I hope there's a toilet on board.'

'It's safer to go in your suit.'

'Go in my suit...'

'I'm joking.'

'Oh...yeah...ha ha.'

Yep, my future self was a funny guy all right. I tried to imagine spending a week stuck in this ship dressed like a bowl of custard.

Oh joy.

So we waited. The boom of the exploding bombs diminished as the ships moved to new territory. Then just as we thought they were gone for good, they returned with a renewed vigor.

I fell asleep. It was almost impossible to tell night from day in this place. Old Axel powered down the craft apart from a few lights. It was continually murky outside. At one point I awoke and found myself looking out at darkness. For one horrifying moment I thought we had drifted into the center of The Eye. Then I heard the crash of distant thunder; the bombs were still falling.

When I opened my eyes next I saw Old Axel had heated some food rations. He and Ebony had their hoods pushed back. I did the same as he handed me a plate. I sniffed it cautiously. It looked like beef. Smelt like beef.

I ate some. Tasted like...

'Is this beef?' I asked.

'No. It's a meat substitute. The Agency has farms in Australia that supply the entire planet.' Old Axel flashed me a rare smile. 'Sure beats that Tagaar food. What was that stuff called. K'trash?'

Ebony and I laughed.

'K'tresh,' Ebony said.

'I remember it fondly,' he said. 'I seem to

recall it tasted like hot seaweed.'

'I don't know,' I said. 'I've never eaten hot seaweed.'

I hadn't meant to make a joke, but the others laughed. I did too when I realized how funny it sounded.

We seemed to be getting along okay. I wanted to ask Old Axel more about the future. More about James Price. More about everything. But there was something I was especially curious about.

'What did you mean when you said we would take revenge on those who have wronged us?' I asked. 'You meant the Agency, don't you?'

His face blackened and he looked down into this food to hide it. 'Don't you worry about that,' he said, pushing his food around. 'Everything will sort itself out if you remove Price from the equation.'

I didn't know what he was trying to hide, but he had a terrible secret. He didn't say anything for a long time. Just kept eating. Finally he put down the plate.

'You don't know who your enemies are when

you're younger,' he said, staring into space. 'You think you can trust everyone.' He broke from his reverie. 'That's why I trust you. Because you're me.'

'You can trust Ebony too,' I pointed out.

'Of course,' he said, forcing a smile. 'Ebony too.'

It felt like the temperature had dropped about ten degrees. We finished eating and resealed our suits. The bombing was drawing closer again. It sounded like there was a pattern to the explosions. The ground shuddered with each detonation. Old Axel looked up, his eyes narrowing.

Another blast, closer than ever, shook the ground.

Pulling down my mask, I formed an air shield around the three of us—and not a moment too soon—as the next bomb landed directly on the ship, tearing it to pieces.

Chapter Thirty-One

My shield saved us, but it was like being in a roller coaster ride with no restraining bar. We were thrown violently into the tempest. I struggled to keep the shield together. When it became obvious we had survived, I pushed up my hood and re-secured it. I started breathing again, but the smell of the storm was in my suit. It was toxic, like burnt rubber. The full blast of the storm hit us.

Ebony grabbed my arm. 'Holy hell!' she said. 'Are you all right?'

I coughed. 'Kind of,' I said. 'The smell—'

'—is revolting,' Old Axel finished. 'I know.'

Another explosion tore the landscape apart, shaking the ground. We saw the flash of it briefly before the storm whisked it away. My eyes settled on Old Axel. He looked the most banged up of the three of us. I actually felt sorry for him.

'I can fly us out,' I said. 'If I get us above the clouds—'

'No. That's plain suicide.'

I bristled. 'I know it's a lot of ships,' I said, 'but I can get us back to Manhattan. I can fly at—'

'I now. Mach Six.' He eyed me carefully. 'You have to pick your fights. This is a time to hide, not to take on the Agency head on.'

'So what will we do?'

He nodded into the wind. 'We walk.'

Old Axel picked up a piece of electrical conduit from the ship and tied us together. Consulting a small compass built into the wrist of the suit, he pointed into the swirling storm.

'East,' he said.

The ground felt like desert underfoot. In fact I had just about made up my mind we had accidentally landed in Death Valley when a multistorey structure loomed in the mist. An office building—or what remained of it. All the glass was missing, leaving only the skeletal structure. In a brief break in the storm I saw another behind it. And another.

Old Axel motioned to a scarred sign.

St Louis Bank, Missouri.

'We've got some distance to cover,' he said.

'We'll take a break first.'

I nodded. He led us to another building, a single story structure with a huge sign scoured clean by the driving wind. The glass in the sliding doors at the front had broken long ago. We passed through into what was once a supermarket, the fog moving about the interior like restless ghosts.

'We should rest,' Old Axel said.

We made our way to the back. Finding a door marked 'Staff', we entered to find the skeletons of two people around a table. Possibly even more disturbing was what lay between them; two glasses, an empty bottle of scotch and a handgun.

Old Axel swept their bodies to one side, untied the rope and went to the door. 'I'll be back in a few minutes.'

'Rough day at the office?' I asked Ebony, after he disappeared.

'The roughest.' She collapsed into the nearest chair. 'I think I slept last night, but I'm not sure.'

'I'm not even sure last night was last night. It's hard to tell in this storm.'

Old Axel appeared with an armful of rotting deck chairs. 'These were on special in aisle seven.'

Ebony laughed. It broke the tension and Old Axel smiled at her. 'I also got us some food,' he said. 'We have to be ready for the days ahead.'

'How do we eat through the suits?' I asked.

Old Axel pulled out a device from a compartment in the suit. It opened up into a huge bag he called the Enclosed Habitation Environment. EHE for short. It closed us off from the outside world. Adjusting a filter on it, he told us to remove our helmets. The air smelt okay. Not great, but good enough.

A few minutes later we were eating beans straight from a can. It tasted like one of the best meals of my life. I started to laugh.

'What's so funny?' Ebony asked.

'Look at us.' I couldn't stop. 'We're living inside a garbage bag.'

'It could be worse,' Ebony said. 'Someone could fart.'

Even Old Axel started laughing.

'I'm serious,' Ebony said, struggling to keep a straight face. 'It could kill us.'

After the meal we donned our helmets again, deflated the EHE and laid out on the three deck chairs. I was asleep almost immediately, awaking some time later to Old Axel shaking my shoulder.

'Come on, sleeping beauty,' he said. 'We need to get moving.'

Ebony was still asleep. He shook her into wakefulness. We had another meal and prepared ourselves for travel. Much to our amazement, Old Axel had already built a makeshift trailer from a shopping trolley, but he had swapped the wheels with bicycle rims. I had no idea how he had put the thing together; he must have been up for hours while we slept.

'You're a resourceful person,' Ebony told him.

Old Axel winked at me. 'We are.'

We set off into the storm. Within minutes we had assumed the same pattern as the previous day. Step after step through the never ending tempest. I began to wish I had not been so committed to my ideals when Old Axel showed up in the time machine. None of this would have happened if I had just agreed to kill James Price.

But that would have been morally wrong. I had known that when I attacked the Russian Premier. That would have been wrong too. Murder was a crime punishable by jail, and with good reason too. Society needed laws or there would be chaos.

I started counting my steps. When I got to one hundred, I started again. It was over eight hundred miles to New York. There would be a lot of counting. I saw a road sign. Interstate 64. Abandoned vehicles lined the road, skeletons a few feet from the cars. I wondered how the end had come for these people. Maybe they were trying to escape the yellow gas when it suffocated them.

All this could be stopped if we killed James Price.

The storm cleared momentarily, revealing a vast rolling plain ahead. My stomach sunk. The highway wasn't visible. Here and there ancient buildings littered the landscape.

Eight hundred miles.

How the hell would we ever survive it?

I dearly wanted to take to the skies. We could be in New York in a matter of minutes if Old Axel allowed it. I would suggest it, but I'd wait a few hours first. He seemed obsessed with keeping me safe, but walking through this storm wasn't the way to do it. He might realize that after a while.

The ground shook. I looked down as a large crack appeared. I could not have been more surprised if an alien ship had landed and John F Kennedy had stepped out.

What the—?

'Run!' Old Axel yelled.

We started forward, but we were already too late. The ground beneath the trailer collapsed first and it vanished from sight. Ebony was next. Then Old Axel. We were still tied to each other. I tried activating my powers, but without success. They would not function properly in the suit. I fell to my knees and made a desperate grab for a tree root, but it snapped in my hand. The last thing I saw was the murky yellow orb of the sun. Then the edge of the ground broke away and I followed the others into darkness.

Chapter Thirty-Two

I slammed into a pile of black dust. It was like landing on a bunch of pillows as it flew in all directions. For a few seconds I couldn't tell up from down. I swam in it. Then I dragged myself free, wiped my hood and peered around.

Ebony was clambering about on the ground a few feet away. It took me a moment to understand she was looking for her hood. I saw it almost immediately. I disconnected myself from our rope system and retrieved it for her. She reconnected it to her suit and I heard her trying to catch her breath.

I realized what had happened: Ebony had saved us. Falling through the hole, she'd dragged off her helmet and turned the air beneath us into carbon dust. We fell about twenty feet, crashed into it and sunk into its depths.

I asked if she was okay.

'Yeah,' she said, coughing. 'I inhaled a few mouthfuls, but I'm all right.'

I went over to Old Axel who had not fared so

well. He had been knocked unconscious by the fall; his head had hit the trolley. I studied his face. At least he was breathing.

'Where are we?' Ebony asked. 'What is this place?'

Storefronts were on both sides of us. A jewelry store. A clothing shop. The center aisle ran away in both directions. Above us was a huge ceiling made from transparent plastic.

'It's a shopping mall,' I said. 'The dust must have covered it over the years. Our weight made the ceiling collapse.'

The wind and the fog screamed over the hole in the roof. Strangely, the air here seemed more breathable, but I wasn't about to test that hypothesis. It was eerily silent after the endless roar of the storm.

'Hello!'

The voice rang out from the gloom where we saw a small man with a torch moving towards us. He waved at us and I cautiously returned the greeting. I could see a thin face, long hair and dark bushy eyebrows. He was not wearing a helmet.

'Visitors!' he said, drawing near. 'We haven't had visitors is such a long time.'

'We fell through your ceiling,' Ebony said.

'So I see. And where did all this coal come from?'

There seemed little point in lying. The man seemed harmless enough. Ebony explained we were mods, trying to make our way back to New York. The man nodded thoughtfully.

'You won't need your helmets down here.' He pointed up. 'We'll send some people back to fix the roof later.'

I peered upwards. Some of the gas was entering, but not a lot. We cautiously removed our helmets. The air was bad, but breathable. Besides, if this man and other people were living down here, it must have been safe.

'We love having visitors,' he said.

Smiling, he reached out and touched our faces. My eyes closed. Somewhere, in the distance, I could hear him laughing. The next thing I knew, I was lying on a bunk in a concrete-lined room. Ebony lay across from me. Our contamination suits were gone. I had no idea what had happened.

'Ebony.' I shook her awake. 'Are you okay?'

She gazed about sleepily. 'What happened? That man—'

'He must be a mod. He knocked us out.'

'You're correct, my young friend.' A slot had opened up in the door leading to the room and a pair of eyes peered in. 'I would like to speak to you.'

'Who are you?' I demanded, angrily jumping to my feet. 'Where is the man who was with us?'

'Your father? He is quite safe.'

I did not correct him.

The stranger continued. 'My name is Jensen. I am going to enter,' he said. 'If you attempt to harm me, there will be repercussions for your father and yourselves. Can we agree to speak like civilized people without the use of violence?'

I felt like pointing out to him violence had already been used against us by knocking us out, and imprisoning us against our will, but I nodded curtly, telling him to come in.

225

'Good,' Jensen said. He was a tall black man, thin with deep recessed eyes. 'Now we can speak in a reasonable manner.'

'What do you want?' I asked. 'Where's my...father?'

'I'm sure you have a million questions, but believe me when I tell you he is safe.'

'Fine,' I said uncertainly. 'We want to see him. Now.'

'That's not immediately possible,' he said. 'There are a few things you must be made aware of first. Then we can discuss terms.'

Terms. I didn't like the sound of that.

'I manage the games. Come with me,' he said. 'Let me show you our home.'

Games. I didn't like *that* word, either.

We followed Jensen down a dark passage lined with locked doors. The end opened up and artificial light flooded in. We entered a wide corridor that led to an underground stadium. Hundreds of seats filled the stands. Crowds were filing in. A show was about to begin.

'What is this?' Ebony asked.

Jensen smiled. 'This facility was owned by the Agency in the old days. James Price had a plan to make genetically modified animals fight to the death. It was abandoned years ago when the ecosystem above become uninhabitable.' He shrugged. 'It's a good life down here. We have nuclear power. Water. Hydroponic farms.' His smile faded. 'But there is never quite enough food. To keep people's minds off starvation, we give them entertainment.

'The city is divided into four quarters: Easterners, Westerners, Northerners and Southerners. Each quarter has several chemically enhanced humans, one of which is chosen each week to compete in the games.'

'The games?'

'It is a fight,' he explained. 'It keeps the people entertained.'

'We just want to get out of here,' I said.

'And you shall. You may have your freedom once you have competed.'

'And if we don't want to compete?' I asked.

'No-one is forcing you to do anything, but it is important that the stakes are high.' He pointed to the stadium's other end where cages perched on top of columns. A person was in each cage. One of them looked familiar. 'High enough to make it interesting,' he said, 'for everyone.'

'That's—'

'Your father. Yes, my boy. He will be killed. The losing team, incidentally, does not receive rations for a week. You will be fighting for the Easterners. They are very hungry right now as their champion was killed last week.'

I gazed up at the cage. Even at this distance I could see the cage was surrounded by glass. A gadget on the top looked like it would release gas into it. I was fast. I could probably be across the stadium in seconds, but I wouldn't be fast enough to save him. Old Axel had proven to be a pain in the ass, but I couldn't let him die.

'You father told us about your powers,' Jensen said. 'You have a good chance of winning.'

I didn't care about playing their stupid game. I

just wanted to escape this crazy place. 'I'll fight,' I said. 'And then we're leaving.'

'Good.' Jensen smiled. 'And remember, my boy, you must fight according to the rules.'

'Which means?'

'It is a fight to the death. Only one of you will leave this stadium alive.'

Chapter Thirty-Three

The siren rang out loud and clear. To me it sounded like the wail of a dying creature as it echoed down the tunnel to where I sat with Ebony. We had been waiting in the preparation room for almost three hours. A guard stood nearby. He nodded to me.

It's time.

I had caught glimpses of two other enhanced humans fighting as we waited. Both had super strength. Soon after, the fight ended and we saw a man being dragged across the stadium to an exit.

There was clearly a difference between enhanced humans and mods. We still looked human, but these people had mutated into something very different. Jensen had explained to us that their powers only lasted a short time. This way the competitors were just as much in the dark about their powers as the audience.

'Stay where I can see you,' I said. 'And be ready for anything.'

Ebony nodded. 'After everything we've been

through,' she said, 'I'm permanently ready for anything.'

I stepped into the stadium. The crowd went crazy. I would have felt like a hero if this whole situation had not been so sick and evil. When I looked closer at the audience, I didn't see the crowd you'd normally find at a football game. These people were malnourished. Starving. This whole society was on the verge of collapse and these games were merely a diversionary tactic to keep them distracted.

'Welcome to the final round of the Sixteenth Games for the year!' a voice boomed from the loud speakers. 'We have a special surprise today as a true mod joins the Easterners.'

The crowd cheered. I could feel hundreds of eyes on me. Strangers down here were a rarity, modified ones more so.

'Today we have a battle of the giants as,' the announcer paused dramatically, '*Easterner* versus *Westerner*!'

The crescendo from the crowd rose even higher in pitch. I was in the midst of the Easterner

231

stands. I could understand their desire for me to win; it meant they could eat for the first time in a week. High up in a podium, I spotted a man speaking into a microphone, obviously the master of ceremonies.

On the other side of the arena, a thin man with gray hair appeared. He bowed to his ecstatic followers, but I could feel him watching me the whole time.

Jensen appeared at my side. 'Good luck, my boy,' he said. 'Your opponent's name is Crenshaw. I'm not sure what they've pumped into him. It's some new concoction they've devised.' He squeezed my arm and nodded to the nearest stand of spectators. 'They are very hungry. Fight well.'

Nodding, I looked across at Crenshaw. I was supposed to kill this man. A complete stranger. There had to be a way out of this—but what?

'Let the games begin!'

I took a single step forward. In that time the stranger had crossed the stadium in a blur and slammed a fist into my chin. My vision blurred as I hit the ground.

Super speed, I thought. *He has super speed.* I urged myself upwards. *Fly. Fly!*

I got into the air. It wasn't easy and I wasn't graceful. Almost unconscious from the single blow, I veered dangerously towards the crowds. People ducked in their seats as I almost slammed into them. Rubbing my chin, I tried to clear my head. That one punch had almost finished me.

Crenshaw was darting about the stadium. I focused on robbing him of oxygen, but he was so fast I couldn't focus on him.

But these people didn't know the extent of my powers. Creating a wall of wind, I slammed it into the arena, hoping to corner him. This time I saw him stumble. The audience screamed and booed. I tried pinning Crenshaw down, but missed him.

He picked up a handful of sand. I saw the whir of an arm and then it was in my eyes. I was twenty feet off the ground and blinded. No sooner had this registered than something slammed into my stomach. I instinctively flew higher as a series of punches smashed into me.

Somehow Crenshaw had made it off the ground. Maybe his powers included flight as well—I had no idea—but I couldn't take this much longer. I created a shield close to my body and pushed Crenshaw away. He fell.

Slowly backing away to the end of the stadium where Old Axel was imprisoned, I was careful to keep my attention on Crenshaw. Forming a tornado of air, I sucked up a mass of sand.

I made it look like I was about to use it as a weapon against the running man. This would take some precision. Making a second flat plane of air, I fired it at Old Axel's cell, destroying the contraption holding the poisonous gas. I released the tornado of air in all directions, blinding most of the audience with sand.

Pulling Old Axel free, we flew over the stadium. Jensen had tried tackling Ebony, but he was no match for her. I saw a solid steel shackles appear around his ankles.

I lifted Ebony up.

'What are you doing?' Old Axel gasped.

'What I should have done in the first place.'

I built up a blast of air and fired it straight into the ceiling. A huge crack appeared. People screamed and began scrambling from their seats. Building up another blast, I smashed it into the ceiling. This time a huge circular gash appeared. I had started a panic in the stands, but I was beyond caring.

I wanted out. And now. I built up another blast and this time the ceiling shattered completely. Beyond lay the endless storm. Gas began to pour into the underground world as I zoomed upwards. I formed a bubble of air around us.

'Hold your breathes,' I yelled.

An instant later we were in the storm, the screaming wind tearing at us. I flew higher, watching the sun, a brown circle of light, grow brighter with each passing second.

Just a little further, I thought. *Just a bit more.*

The terrible yellow cloud cleared and we flew into crystal clean air. I whooped and laughed. Ebony cried out and waved her arms about. Even Old Axel looked momentarily relieved. Still, he couldn't stop himself from souring the moment.

'You shouldn't have done that,' he said. 'The skies are probably still full of Agency ships.'

'Good,' I told him. 'I'm counting on it.'

Chapter Thirty-Four

I was sick of running. I was sick of hiding. I wanted to be back in my own time. I wanted to be away from this twisted future.

But first we needed a ship. My eyes scanned the horizon, making out a tiny dot.

'Hold on,' I said. 'I've got to be fast if this is going to work.'

I had done everything Old Axel's way. I had followed his rules. Taken his advice. I had hidden when I wanted to fight. Well, no more. Now I was doing it my way. I sped across the sky, catching up to the ship in seconds. Veering under it, I kept pace for a few seconds.

'Oxygen!' I yelled at Ebony.

She appeared momentarily confused, but nodded. A second later I brought us up in front of the craft and plastered us against the window.

'Now!' I yelled.

She evaporated the glass and then we were inside the control cabin with the two pilots. They were taken completely by surprise. Possibly they had been trying to track my path when we dropped in their laps. I knocked them out, dumping them into a rear cell.

Ebony reformed the glass as Old Axel took control of the ship.

'That was amazing,' he said.

'Thanks.'

'Insane, but amazing. It was stupid to risk your life like that.'

'Yeah,' I said. 'Like we were already in a safe place.'

Ebony gave me a friendly punch to the arm. 'Well,' she laughed. '*I* thought you were amazing.'

I winced. 'Sorry, that's—'

'Oops. The fight. Forgot about that.'

I wished I could. Now that I had a moment to relax, I realized I was in a world of pain. Easing myself into the navigator's seat, Ebony fetched painkillers from the first aid kit. I swallowed a few while I assessed where I hurt the most. It was hard to pick. My jaw felt terrible. A couple of my ribs were cracked.

'I feel awful,' I groaned.

'Relax for a while,' Old Axel said. 'I might have some good news for you.'

'Good. I need some.'

'I'm signaling to the other Agency ships that we're having problems with our engines and we're returning to base.' He smiled at us. 'We're going home in style.'

'Thanks to me,' I said.

'Thanks to all of us,' he replied.

I fell back, exhausted. The last few days had been insane. After this I was taking a holiday. I would lie down on a beach and not move for a week. I closed my eyes. When I opened them again I heard Old Axel talking.

'Wassat?' I said.

'I'm getting a signal on a secure channel,' he said. 'Encrypted.'

'From the Agency?' I sat up.

'No. It's a branch of the resistance.'

'How is that possible?' I asked. 'No-one even

239

knows we have this ship.'

'It's being sent on a channel used by an East coast group,' Old Axel explained. 'They're sending a set of coordinates.'

'What are you going to do?'

Old Axel glared at the console. 'We'll go,' he said, his jaw hardening. 'We don't really have a choice.'

'Why not?'

He didn't answer. Ebony and I exchanged a glance. There was something he wasn't telling us. Within minutes we were zooming over a mist filled town west of Washington. After landing us in an alley near a statue of some founding father, Old Axel retrieved some contamination suits from the back lockers.

'Who was sending that signal?' Ebony asked.

Old Axel swallowed. 'I'm not sure.'

'But you have a pretty good idea.'

'I know who's used it in the past.'

'Who?'

He refused to answer. Leaving the ship, we

found ourselves in a fog enshrouded street in a typical town in middle America. A tall building with a tower lay across the road from us. The streets were quiet though. The gas was as poisonous here as the mid-west.

We climbed the steps, Old Axel pushed the doors open and entered a town hall with paintings of various civic leaders lining the walls. Surprisingly, the interior was in pretty good condition with most of the old woodwork intact. We continued on to the council chambers. Some sort of high tech plastic lay across the doors, creating an airlock. We pushed through.

'Axel!' Brodie screamed.

She jumped up from a seat near the lectern. Chad followed close behind and we found ourselves in a group hug. There had been times over the last few days that I thought I'd never see my friends again. It was like coming home. Old Axel crossed to some people in the corner. I ignored them for the moment as we exchanged stories.

We had brought each other up to date when I

sensed something was wrong. Chad looked worried while Brodie kept glancing over my shoulder. Finally I turned to take a closer look.

Four people stood there. My mouth dropped open as I recognized the older versions of Brodie and Chad. This was getting weirder and weirder. A red-headed girl stood with them and Old Axel. The girl was eyeing our group as the adults engaged in some sort of heated discussion. She was young like us.

I had never seen her before, but she was familiar.

Why?

Something was wrong here. Horribly wrong. I felt it in the pit of my stomach. It was like playing a game of chess and knowing I was a move away from checkmate.

'What's going on?' I asked. 'Who's that girl?'

'I think they're catching up on lost time,' Brodie said, airily. 'They haven't seen each other for years.'

She was deliberately ignoring my question.

'And the girl?'

Neither of them spoke.

'Who's the girl?' I asked again.

'She's their daughter,' Chad said, his face reddening. 'Their future daughter.'

Their future daughter? He was speaking some kind of foreign language. It didn't make any sense. I muttered something incomprehensible and then it clicked in my mind and I understood. *Their future daughter.* Now I looked at the girl again and I knew why she was familiar.

Brodie was speaking, but I couldn't hear her. *Their future daughter.* She was Chad and Brodie's *future* daughter. Now all the pieces were falling into place. This was what Old Axel didn't want to tell me.

...contaminate the time line, causing irreparable damage to the space/time continuum...

My relationship with Brodie wasn't going to last.

...take revenge upon those who have wronged us...

She was destined to fall in love with Chad.

...you think you can trust everyone...

243

But my friends would betray me.

'—one of those weird time line things,' Brodie was saying. 'It doesn't mean anything.'

I had missed most of what she'd said. 'Your future daughter. Wow. That must have been a surprise.' I managed to keep my voice under control. Almost. A tiny look of relief crossed Chad's face, but I wasn't fooling Brodie. She knew me too well.

'Please,' she said quietly. 'It's nothing, I promise.'

Sure it was nothing. *To them.* But they weren't the ones who'd been betrayed.

I was.

'Why would it mean anything to you?' I asked, my voice rising. 'My best friend and my girlfriend end up together, so what does that make me?'

'Hey man,' Chad started. 'You've got to understand—'

'*I thought you were my friends!*'

The wind began to build in the chamber. The group in the corner stopped speaking as a minitornado formed around me. I pushed everyone away. Chad. Brodie. Even Ebony. She was Chad's sister. Did she already know about this? I didn't know or care.

I couldn't be with people I didn't trust.

I was so enraged I didn't hear the doors fly open behind me. It was only when Ebony fell that I knew something was happening. Looking back, I saw men in combat suits firing stun weapons at us. I tried to react, but I was already too late. A man had me firmly in his sights. He pulled the trigger and everything went black.

Chapter Thirty-Five

A ceiling went racing by. Two men were holding my arms, dragging me down a corridor. I tried using my powers, but nothing happened so I fought against them. I saw one of them raise a baton and everything went dark again.

A million years passed—or so it seemed. When I next awoke, I found myself on a concrete floor with something around my neck. A brace of some kind. I blearily looked about, my eyes finally focusing on Chad.

'It's a portable zeno ray generator,' he informed me. 'Our powers are kaput.'

'Great,' I mumbled, peering around the cell. Brodie and Ebony were hunched together against a wall. 'Where are the others?'

Ebony spoke up. 'They were taken somewhere else.'

The room was concrete with a single barred window. Very Twentieth century. By comparison, the door was some sort of force field, transparent except for a red haze.

'I already tried it,' Chad said, holding up a burnt finger. 'Ouch.'

Beyond lay an empty hallway with elevators at the other end. I tried in vain to push the wall down, but it was pointless. Chad was right. The brace was designed to nullify our powers and it was working. I tried tearing it off with pure brute force, but to no avail. These things had been keeping mods under control for decades.

I glanced at Brodie. Whoever had imprisoned us knew our powers intimately. She had been secured to the wall with a metal brace. I caught her eye momentarily, but then I remembered what the future held for Chad and Brodie. Happy families. Together forever. The wrenching apart of everything I'd known since I'd woken up in a squalid hotel room with superpowers. I looked away.

Despite the terrible situation we were in, I could understand why Old Axel was so bitter and angry. He—or I—had been betrayed by my closest friends.

'Someone's coming,' Ebony said.

The elevator doors slid open. Two guards approached with a man behind. He had gray hair and a youthful face. What was it Old Axel had said?

The years—and plastic surgery—have been kind to him.

The door dissolved and Price stepped in. The guards produced weapons, aiming them at us. They didn't stop Chad. He immediately made a grab for Price, but a bolt of crackling electricity from a weapon knocked him down.

Writhing in agony, unable to stand, he spat at Price through clenched teeth. 'You're going to regret that,' he said.

'I doubt it,' James Price said. He had a high-pitched voice, belying his callous interior. Turning to a guard, he said, 'Again.'

So they hit Chad with another bolt. We leapt to our feet, but the guards waved us back.

'I can make things very bad for you,' Price said. 'You don't want that. Not yet.'

Ebony dragged Chad away where he crouched

against her, shaking, blood seeping from a cut in his mouth.

'What's going to happen to us?' she asked.

'I'm a scientist. I want to know what makes you tick,' he said. 'I've experimented on a lot of mods over the years. There's always more to learn.'

'You're sick,' I said.

He laughed. 'After I've found out what I want, you will be neutered, your powers permanently removed. Then I will confine you to the lowest levels of the darkest dungeon I can find, and there you will rot for the remainder of your lives.'

I tried to think of something clever to say, but nothing came.

'Nor will your older selves ever see the light of day again,' he continued. 'You've had a wonderful adventure, but your days of adventuring are over. As the years slowly pass, I'm sure you will remember those times fondly, hoping you will one day escape.' Price shook his head sadly. 'But you never will.'

He marched out, the guards reactivated the door and they disappeared into the elevator.

'And here I was thinking this was serious,' Chad said.

No-one laughed.

We remained silent for over an hour, lost in our own thoughts, drowned by the horror of what James Price had said.

Finally Brodie muttered something under her breath.

'What?' I asked.

'That's Morse code.'

Brodie could have said the moon was made from green cheese and it would have made more sense. She pointed at the light. It had been flickering on and off for several minutes, but I had barely noticed it.

'What's Morse code?' Chad asked.

'An old kind of message system using dots and dashes. The light is sending a message.'

I stared at her.

'It is!' she continued, angrily. 'It's saying...E...L...E...V...' A few seconds passed. 'Elevator. It's saying elevator.'

I nodded. 'Sure.'

A click came from my throat and I felt the brace loosening. Gingerly touching it, I pulled it away in amazement. I stared at the others. Theirs had also unlocked.

'What's going on?' Chad asked.

'No idea,' Ebony replied. 'But I don't care. Let's go.'

I crossed to Brodie and broke her metal chains. I was still pissed with her and Chad, but we had to focus on getting out of here. With a little effort I could smash a hole in the wall—

The red haze in the doorway flickered to static before it faded completely.

'Do you get the feeling someone's helping?' Brodie asked.

'Maybe it's a trap,' Ebony said.

'Shot while trying to escape?' I said. 'They don't need to do that. They could have killed us anytime they wanted

We made our way to the elevator. It appeared as if almost on cue. Climbing in, we stood, undecided, until the elevator made up its mind for us. It descended. I should have been rejoicing in our newfound freedom, but instead an image of Chad and Brodie together flashed through my mind, and acid burnt in my stomach as we sunk into the bowels of the earth.

Chapter Thirty-Six

The elevator slowed to a halt, opening onto a fifty-foot-high concrete hallway. Florescent lighting lined the ceiling, but most of the tubes were dead, leaving an odd checkerboard of light and shadow to illuminate our way.

'What is this place?' Ebony asked.

'I think this whole compound is an old Agency stronghold,' Brodie replied. 'This area must have been abandoned.'

'It doesn't look like it's been used in years,' Chad agreed.

The corridor seemed endless, but we finally reached a door at the end that opened onto a chamber with huge computers on each side. They were ancient; the type that still operated on magnetic reels of tape, like they used last century. Incredibly, they were still operational, doing...*something*.

'This is bizarre,' Ebony said.

She said it. Benches were everywhere, dust covering the surfaces. A coffee cup even sat on one, the liquid inside long since evaporated. The controls on the benches were ancient. Buttons and levers. Like us, they were something from another time.

'What are we doing here?' I asked. 'And who sent us that code?'

'Over there,' Brodie said, pointing to a light flashing over a door. 'That wasn't on before.'

The door gave a huge squeak as I pulled it open. Beyond was another chamber, even older and bigger than the last. A row of light bulbs were set into the ceiling; most had blown over the years, but a few yellowing globes still provided a faint illumination. No-one had been here in decades.

A massive computer several hundred feet in length dominated one side. Colored lights flashed. Hundreds of reels whirred and clicked. The machine appeared so old it looked like it had been built as part of the building. I had seen a photo of a similar device in an book; some of the early computers had taken up entire floors because of their size. This one was larger. Maybe it was the largest in its day.

A faint monitor glowed in the dark. We

studied the screen. A green cursor blinked. It could have been doing that for ages. Maybe years.

'This is a dead end,' Chad said. 'We have to get out of here.'

'I agree,' Ebony said, peering about the darkened recesses. 'I appreciate that someone released us, but now we've got to escape while the going's good.'

We started combing the room for an exit, but came up empty handed. There wasn't even an air vent in the chamber. We were at the lowest level of a bunker set deep into the earth.

So why had someone brought us here? My eyes returned to the monitor.

'Hang on,' I said, staring at the screen. 'This has changed.'

The others came over and peered over my shoulder.

The letter *W* had appeared.

A distant rumble came from far away. Chad ran from the room, returning a minute later. 'A bunch of Agency guards just came pouring out of the elevator,' he said. 'They don't look happy.'

I turned back to the screen.

A

'You've got to stop them,' I told Chad. 'Or at least slow them down.'

'What are you going to do?'

'Someone brought us here for a reason. We've got to find out why.'

Ebony grabbed Chad's arm. 'I'll come with you.'

More letters appeared.

I

T

'WAIT,' Brodie read the word. 'Wait for what?'

A massive fight erupted in the hallway leading to the chamber.

The word started flashing.

Wait. Wait. Wait.

A breeze pulled at my hair. I looked about in surprise. This room had no windows so there could be no wind. Then the current grew stronger as a tiny black line appeared in the middle of the room, growing larger as a strange hum filled the air.

'What the hell..?' Brodie's mouth fell open in amazement. 'How—'

I didn't know how. It made no sense at all, but now the line had expanded into a circle and we could see a small silver vessel inside. Within seconds it had eased itself free from the portal in time and space.

'It's a time machine,' I said.

The vessel shuddered slightly, dropping to the floor. Pieces of ice fell off and smashed. I raced over and jerked the door open. Empty. No-one was flying it. Stepping back from the craft, I saw it was smaller than the one in which we had traveled to the future. Possibly it was an earlier model.

An earlier model.

It all clicked into place.

I raced to the console. The word on the screen had disappeared and another had appeared while we examined the time machine. I barked out a laugh of disbelief.

It wasn't possible and yet somehow it all

made sense.

Ferdy. Ferdy. Ferdy.

Chapter Thirty-Seven

'Dan?' the voice came from a million miles away. 'Dan?'

Dan awoke slowly, opened his eyes and saw Henry standing over him.

'Henry?'

'Are you all right?' Henry asked. 'Did the monster hurt you?'

Holding onto Henry for support, Dan pulled himself upright and peered around. *Liber8tor* lay at a crazy angle. Miraculously, a few consoles were back online, as was the emergency lighting.

'The monster didn't hurt me,' Dan said. 'But it hurt our ship.'

And I helped it, he thought. *Because I was hopeless.*

'The monster's bad,' Henry said, his face crumpling into tears. 'He's bad and Henry just wants to be good.'

'I'm sure you do.' Dan gripped the boy's shoulder. He had wrecked the ship, but now he had to move forward. That's what the others would do. They would take stock and find a way to make things better. 'We're going to beat it,' he promised, 'but first I've got to fix our ship.'

He crossed to the navigation console. 'Ferdy? Can you hear me?'

Silence.

Great, Dan thought. *Ferdy's still offline. Or broken. Or dead.*

No, he couldn't think that way. *Liber8tor* was tough and Ferdy was too. Ferdy was probably fine, but unable to communicate because of the damage. Dan manually brought up a status report of the systems, thankful for the time he had put in learning the Tagaar language. The words he couldn't read, he was able to guess. The system seemed to be rebooting itself.

'How did you get in?' he asked Henry.

'The hatch downstairs is broken.'

Hell, Dan thought. *I'd better check the outer hull.*

He retrieved a weapon from the Tagaar

armory. They had not used these since they had taken over the ship; having superpowers made them superfluous. However, Dan's last encounter with the monster had shaken his confidence. He wasn't going outside without firepower.

Henry trailed him as Dan carefully surveyed the damage. The port side had taken quite a bang. Much of the housing was damaged, but his ability to manipulate metal would easily fix it.

The most difficult task would be to repair the engines. One of the firing thrusters was completely smashed. An oily black liquid leaked from a cracked pipe. Something Dan couldn't even identify was completely crushed. Peering into the mess, he understood how little he actually knew about the ship. For that matter, none of them knew anything much about it. They relied upon Ferdy to keep the ship's systems operational.

Dan promised himself he would change that. He would become an expert in every square inch of this ship, as long as he was given the chance. Although considering what he had done to *Liber8tor* during their absence, the others might permanently confine him to quarters.

Dan frowned. He was getting ahead of himself. One thing at a time.

'This looks bad,' he said to Henry, 'but I think it's fixable.'

'So your ship will fly again?'

'Yes, but I've got to get Ferdy up and running.' He glanced down and noticed Henry still had his book tightly clenched in his hand. 'You're still reading your book?'

'I read it all the time.'

'Do you remember anything more about how you came to the island? The ship you were on? Your parents?'

'No.'

'What's the first thing you remember?'

Henry creased his brow in concentration. 'I just remember waking up on the island,' he said. 'I looked down and saw I was holding my book.'

That wasn't very helpful, so Dan gripped his shoulder. 'Everything will be all right,' he said. 'My friends will be back soon and we'll get you back to civilization.'

A distant roar came from the jungle. Henry grabbed Dan's arm in panic, his eyes filling with tears. 'It's the monster,' he said. 'We should run away.'

'We'll be okay aboard *Liter8tor*.'

Henry gazed dubiously at the wrecked ship.

'I know that's hard to believe,' Dan said. 'Just let me take a look at this damaged pipe and we'll go inside.'

He examined the broken pipe more closely. It was a hydraulic system. Taking a handkerchief from his pocket, he wrapped it around the break. It didn't stop the leak, but it slowed.

'That's better already,' he said. 'Henry?'

The boy was gone.

Dan moaned in frustration, but he could understand Henry's fear. *Liber8tor* hardly looked like a safe refuge. He did a check inside the ship anyway, but Henry was definitely gone. Returning to the bridge, Dan called out Ferdy's name.

He was greeted by silence. Then—

'Ferdy can hear you!'

Yes!

'Ferdy!' Dan cried. 'How are you feeling?'

'Ferdy is feeling fine, but a number of the *Liber8tor* systems were damaged in the crash.'

'Uh, yeah. Sorry about that.'

'Dan should not blame himself. Whatever was stopping *Liber8tor* from leaving the island was a powerful force. Dan did well to stop the ship from being destroyed.'

'Thanks,' Dan said, embarrassed at the praise. 'Hey, I saw Henry again.'

'That is good.'

'But now he's missing again. I think he was scared about the monster returning to the ship.'

'That is understandable,' Ferdy agreed. 'Also, Charles Chaplin Senior was also a famous performer long before his son—'

It sounded like Ferdy was returning to normal. 'Henry and I shouldn't have left *Liber8tor*,' Dan said, thoughtfully. 'Then he wouldn't have heard the monster in the jungle.'

Ferdy didn't reply.

'Ferdy,' Dan said. 'Are you still there?'

'Ferdy is still here. Is Dan saying Henry was onboard *Liber8tor*?'

'He was on the ship when I woke up after the crash.'

'That is not possible.'

Dan frowned. 'Huh?'

'*Liber8tor* tracks heat signatures of life forms aboard the ship. No new entries have been added to the log.'

'The system must have been broken,' Dan said.

'That particular system has been fully operational the whole time. The only person who has been on board *Liber8tor* is Dan.'

'That's crazy,' Dan said. 'You're telling me Henry is some kind of—'

He didn't dare say the word.

Ghost.

Chapter Thirty-Eight

'There must be something wrong with the ship,' Dan insisted.

'Many of *Liber8tor*'s systems were offline, but that particular component is part of life support. It was working normally.' Ferdy paused. 'Is Dan sure that he didn't imagine the experience?'

Dan felt his stomach churning. He *had* been rattled after the crash, but he was awake. He was sure of it. 'I need to find Henry,' he said. 'I'm going out looking for him.'

'Ferdy does not think that is a good idea. The entity that attacked *Liber8tor* was extremely dangerous.'

But Dan wouldn't listen. His gut was churning. He was the only person who had actually seen Henry. Could the boy have been a figment of his imagination *the whole time*?

Pocketing the Tagaar blaster, he filled his backpack with metal pipes and checked his communicator was still working as he headed to the exit. 'Can you keep repairing the *Liber8tor* systems?' he asked Ferdy. 'And try to find out what this island was used for during the war.'

'Ferdy will do what he can. And one more thing, friend Dan.'

'Yes,' Dan said, ready for Ferdy to pass on some useless information about the life cycle of bees, or the size of the planet Jupiter. 'What is it?'

'Be careful.'

'Oh. Thank you. Yes, I will.'

Dan headed in the direction of the buildings. He was afraid of the monster that lived on this island, but he was even more afraid for his own sanity. Could he have imagined Henry? No. Was Henry a ghost? Dan wasn't sure he believed in ghosts. The sensors on board *Liber8tor* had to be faulty. He had touched Henry. Felt him. He was real.

He remembered the wrecked ship on the beach and changed direction. Minutes later he was climbing aboard the *Morning Star*, calling out Henry's name. No greeting came back, but he hadn't expected the boy to be here anyway. Dan returned to the room where he had found the skeletal remains, grimacing as he examined the bones more closely. There was no doubt about it. They were the bodies of two adults. Dan continued to the next cabin. He had not come this far last time. The wild pig had scared him off. Now he pushed open a door and peered into a darkened cabin.

This was another bunk room containing four beds. Two on each side. The bedding had long since deteriorated to muck. Some of it on one bed looked like it had been eaten, probably by the pig. A white shape poked out from under a bed.

He cautiously peered under it—and grimaced. Another skeleton. A skull was mixed in with a tangle of bones and clothing. The remains were that of a small child. Presumably Henry's brother, Charles. Dan started to rise from the floor, but then he saw something that stopped him.

'No,' he said. 'That's not possible.'

Under the opposite bunk were more bones. A second child.

'How is that possible?' Dan asked aloud. He snapped on his communicator. 'Ferdy, do you read me?'

'Loud and clear, friend Dan.'

'How many people were on the *Morning Star* when it went missing?'

'Four.'

'Have you found out anything more about the Japanese on this island?'

'Ferdy is still gathering information.' He went on to say that seventy percent of the ship's systems were back online. The engine still needed repairs, but he had formulated a plan to make the ship fully operational again. '*Liber8tor* will be ready for travel within twenty-four hours.'

Stomping back into the jungle, Dan made his way to the settlement, returning to the long corridor of cells.

'Henry?'

The small boy was back in the last cell. He raised his head over the rubble. 'Dan?' he said, tears in his eyes. 'I was scared.'

'Everything's okay,' Dan said, holding him tightly. Henry was as warm blooded as himself. 'We'll be away from here before you know it.' His communicator crackled to life. 'Ferdy?'

'Hello Dan. Ferdy has discovered some more information regarding Doctor Hiroto Satou and his research.'

'What is it?'

'It seems his later research involved fungi.'

'Fungi?'

'Molds, mildew, mushrooms—'

'Anything else?'

'Not yet, Dan. The *Liber8tor* computer system is now fully repaired.'

Good old Ferdy, Dan thought. *Where would we be without him?*

He thanked him and signed off. Looking down at Henry, he saw the boy was still holding his book. 'Do you mind if I see that?'

Henry handed the book to him. Dan leafed through it. The novel was a worn out volume, and quite old, dating to the middle of last century. The lines were quite close together, a strange book for a small boy to be reading. Dan supposed it was the only—

His eyes froze on a page.

'Henry,' Dan said. 'What's your last name?'

'Jekyll,' Henry said, looking at him with innocent round eyes. 'My name is Henry Jekyll.'

Henry Jekyll was the name of the protagonist in Henry's book.

Dr Jekyll and Mr Hyde.

Chapter Thirty-Nine

A low growl emanated from the corridor's far end. Henry grabbed Dan's hand. 'Don't leave me, Dan,' he pleaded. 'I'm afraid.'

'I won't leave you,' Dan promised.

A shape moved in the dark, a large, shifting mass that Dan had last seen in the cave. Now Dan focused on it and realized it looked more human than he had first thought, a man made taller by what appeared to be a long coat and hat, but still more shadow than solid.

'Who are you?' Dan yelled. 'What do you want?'

The figure started towards them, and Dan pulled out the gun, aiming it.

'Stay where you are or I'll shoot!' It continued to advance. 'I warned you.'

Dan fired. The blast hit the creature and it stumbled, the point of impact exploding into millions of tiny particles, leaving a huge gap in its shape. The particles scattered into the air like flies before returning to the form and filling the hole. Dan fired again. And again. Each time the figure stumbled before repairing itself.

'Dan!' Henry pulled at his arm. 'We've got to go!'

Dan wanted to run, but he wasn't ready. Not yet. 'I know who you are,' Dan said to the approaching figure. 'You're Mr. Hyde.'

He fired again, then grabbed Henry's hand and dragged him up the debris to the jungle. Pushing the boy ahead, he was almost over the edge when the creature grabbed his leg, dragging him back down the slope. The smell of the creature struck him again, the same terrible stench of mold and decay. Dan aimed at the creature's arm, fired again and the limb dissolved into mist.

Rolling, Dan narrowly avoided its other hand as it came smashing down into the debris.

'Leave him alone!' The voice came from above, and Dan saw Henry standing at the edge of the hole. 'He's my friend!' Henry yelled. 'You leave him alone!'

Dan squirmed free and scrambled down the corridor, adjusting a setting on the weapon designed to disperse the beam over a wider area. Glancing back, he saw the creature had frozen, undecided whether it should pursue him or Henry.

Dan pulled the trigger again. This time everything from the shoulders up was reduced to nothing.

What remained of the monster—everything from the waist down—blindly staggered about in confusion as something flitted past Dan. A transparent black cloud raced to the monster. At first a faint outline appeared, then it grew more solid, rebuilding the body in seconds.

The monster flexed its hands, focusing on Dan and started towards him. Firing again, Dan smashed another hole in it. More of the tiny black particles floating past him. He inhaled. They smelt like mold.

Dan gasped. Doctor Hiroto Satou's later research had been in fungus and *mold was a kind of fungus.*

Dan turned and ran to the cell with the huge

patch of mold growing across the back wall. The monster roared in fury, but Dan already had the gun pointed at the fungus. He jerked the trigger and the mold burst into flames.

Bellowing a blood-curdling cry, the monster staggered and fell to its knees. It tried crawling towards Dan, but didn't make it. The millions of black particles dispersed. Henry appeared beyond it, taking a single faltering step before collapsing.

'Henry!' Dan yelled.

He cradled the small boy in his arms, not understanding how any of this had happened, but knowing that whatever Henry was, he was innocent. He had simply wanted to *be*.

Henry's skin turned brown as he became as light as a feather.

'I've tried to be good,' he said.

'You *are* good,' Dan said, his face wet with tears. 'You're a good boy.'

Henry nodded and didn't speak again. His head fell back. He dissolved into dust, and then less than dust, and then Dan was holding only the memory of him. Dan picked up the book and went back to the cell where the mold had been growing. The fire was still burning fiercely. In the midst of the flames lay a skeleton wearing the remnants of a United States navy uniform.

Forcing the doors open, Dan tossed the book into the flames.

'Goodbye Henry,' he said.

Chapter Forty

'Get the others,' I yelled.

Brodie raced from the room as I climbed into the time ship. I quickly swapped an old temporal resonator with a new. Focusing on the controls, I saw they were similar to those Old Axel had used on the other machine. The date was easy; I set it for the time and date we had departed. Getting the coordinates for our departure location was harder, but I managed it just as Chad and the others burst through the door. Squeezing into the tight compartment, they slammed the hatch shut.

'I've thrown up a wall of ice,' Chad said, 'but they'll be through it in a minute. There's a mod out there—'

I started the time ship. As the vessel rose, I activated the firing sequence and a portal appeared. I aimed us into it as a bunch of guards broke through into the underground chamber and started firing. They were too late. The ship started its descent down the time corridor.

'Does someone want to explain what's going on?' Chad asked. 'Where did this time ship come from? And who sent it to us?'

'Ferdy,' I said. 'His name flashed on the console screen at the last minute.'

'Ferdy?' Ebony said. 'But he's dead. Old Axel said he was killed years ago.'

I had already been thinking about this. 'Ferdy wasn't killed,' I said. 'I think he's been hiding in the bowels of the Agency computer system all these years.'

'But the time machine?' Ebony said. 'How—'

'It was sent to us by Ferdy. You remember Old Axel said several of the machines went missing while they were being tested? I bet you that was no accident. One of them was this machine.'

'That's stupid,' Chad said. 'How could he know we'd get captured by James Price?'

'You remember Ferdy saying he can perceive possible futures? This was probably one, a future where my older self went to the past and asked for our help. It's not too hard to guess that we'd want evidence.'

Ebony was nodding. 'Like seeing the future for ourselves.'

'Exactly. And that we might get captured and brought to Agency headquarters.'

The time machine shuddered as a distant patch of blue appeared. It was growing larger by the second. Before I could speak, it rushed towards us and then we were through and sailing across a clear sky. I hadn't gotten our coordinates completely right. We were about three miles away west of the island.

'Looks like Dan's been busy,' Brodie said.

The *Liber8tor* was lying at the edge of the clearing, one side damaged as if an elephant had rammed it. Dan was working on it with a toolkit at his feet.

'At least he doesn't look ten years older,' Chad said. 'You know, like we've arrived ten years later than we left.

Chad was trying to lighten the mood, but I wasn't laughing.

After bringing the ship in to an untidy landing,

we silently made our way back to *Liber8tor*. The resentment within me was still sour, like curdled milk. I knew the future now. Brodie would dump me. She and Chad would be together. Forever. The joke was on me.

Dan looked up at us. 'Hey team!' he yelled. 'You wouldn't believe what happened!'

'You got drunk and crashed *Liber8tor*?' Brodie asked.

'No. There was a boy named Henry, but he wasn't really a boy. And there was a monster and it was like a—'

'Hold on,' Ebony said. 'Let's grab a meal and you can tell us all about it.'

The others headed inside, but I grabbed Brodie. We needed to speak.

'Do you want to explain to me about Chad?' I asked.

'I don't know what you mean.' She looked furious. 'Don't tell me you're still annoyed. Your older self was right. We're better off not knowing our futures.'

'I'm not talking about *our* future,' I said. 'I'm talking about the present. How do I know you're not running around with Chad?'

A shadow crossed her face.

'What?' I said. 'Tell me.'

'It's not important. It doesn't mean anything.'

Some people can keep secrets, but Brodie isn't one of them. She haltingly told me about her illness and Chad saving her. She didn't look me in the eye as she related everything that had happened. Everything including the kiss.

I felt the world drop out from under me.

Chad had kissed Brodie.

I heard the fall of footsteps. Chad spoke, but I didn't hear it. Rage blinded me as I drew back a fist and slammed it into his face. He fell backwards into *Liber8tor*'s hull.

'What do you think you're doing?' he screamed.

'You've been running around with Brodie!'

He stared at me with a mixture of guilt and confusion. 'You've never loved her,' he said. 'So why do you care?'

Brodie yelled as we flew at each other. Within seconds we were rolling about on the ground, threatening to tear each other's heads off. Ebony and Dan raced out of *Liber8tor*. It took the three of them to drag us apart.

'Stop! Stop!' Brodie screamed, tears running down her face. 'We're friends! We have to stick together!'

'I don't have any friends!' I yelled, leaping into the air.

Brodie screamed my name as I flew away from the island, but I kept going. I had a mission to complete. I had to kill James Price.

Chapter Forty-One

I flew across the Pacific filled with a rage unlike anything I had ever known. The skies were clear at first, but then a storm appeared on the horizon. I had flown through bad weather before, but never through anything like this. It dominated most of the skyline. Any other time I would have flown around it, but this time I drove straight into its heart.

The thin pocket of air I always kept around my body deflected the rain, but I could still feel the effects of the wind as it tore at me. This was a massive tempest with winds pulling in all directions, thunder rolling like the ringing of an enormous bell.

I thought about Brodie and I thought about Chad, but mostly I thought about James Price. How many people were dead because of him? Billions? The world would be a better place if he were not part of it. It was wrong to kill one man, but even worse to allow wholesale slaughter.

Lightning flashed, the hair stood up on my arms and a moment later a bolt of energy crackled and danced around me. It was as if I was at the storm's heart, as much a part of nature's unbridled power as the rain and the wind.

And then I was through. Soaring away from it, I looked back at the bubbling mass of energy as it heaved and writhed like a living thing. The lightning continued to flash, but I was separate from it. Disgorged from its belly and alone in the world.

An hour later, I reached the west coast of the United States. I was still visible to radar, but I wasn't worried. The government—or the Agency—wouldn't scramble any fighters. So many mods were flying about these days that it was impossible to tell one from another.

I didn't know where James Price was located so I flew into the Los Angeles area to do what anyone else would have done: I found an internet cafe. It didn't take long for me to find his New York address, and take to the skies again.

Night fell as I landed in the heart of the country. I had been here the previous day—and forty years in the future—when it would be a desolate wasteland. This was where the eye of an eternal storm would lay waste to the country. Arriving here again reminded me of the purpose of my mission. The night was clear and quiet as I booked into a rundown motel in Missouri, not far from Route Sixty-Six. The woman gave me an odd look as I asked for a room.

'You're traveling by yourself,' she said.

'Yes, ma'am.'

'Aren't you a little young fer that?'

The adventures I'd had over the last few months, including my latest foray into the future, would have turned her hair gray. She was better off not knowing. Paying for a single night, I told her I was meeting my parents in the morning.

The view out the window of the room was of the parking lot. A man went to his car and drove off. I heard someone playing country music on a radio. An insect buzzed in the night. The motel's neon sign flashed on and off. A car pulled in, a couple got out and went to their room, but not before tossing their empty beer cans into the bushes.

This was not a perfect world.

I awoke early with my head throbbing from a night of tossing and turning. The events of the last few days had kept me awake half the night. My thoughts went from the fight with Chad to imagining he and Brodie together. Laughing at me behind my back. Brodie had said it was just a kiss, but how could I know for sure?

How long had he felt this way about her? Had he always been planning this? Did everyone know what was going on—except me?

Leaping into the sky, I continued towards New York, catching sight of its distinctive skyline within hours. I had been here forty years from now when it would lie in ruins.

Changing direction towards Staten Island, I descended into a small suburb made up of family homes, parks and quiet streets. James Price's street was closed to traffic at one end. His home was a timber clad, barn style building with a pitched roof. The driveway was empty. Possibly he had left for an early morning drive.

I waited.

Children were leaving for school. A young mother walked up the street holding hands with son. She glanced at me curiously. Maybe they didn't see too many strangers on this street. I forced a friendly smile, but my stomach was turning over with tension. I had already faced a dilemma like this; I had come very close to using a weapon on the Russian Premier that would have consigned him to a fate worse than death.

This time I would be killing someone. Committing the act of murder. Snuffing out their life forever. I supposed there were people I had killed in battle, but that was unavoidable. They had wanted to kill me and so I had defended myself.

This was a completely different thing. This was premeditated murder.

But was it so different? I knew what the future held; James Price would be responsible for the deaths of billions of people. He was one person. One life. One man's life couldn't be balanced against all the others.

Could it?

Except, he hadn't actually committed any crimes. As far as I knew, he was an innocent man. I was judging him prior to doing anything and finding him guilty. Except he *was* guilty. That future would unfold if he wasn't stopped now.

My head ached, the stress at the back of my neck like a tightly coiled snake. I wandered up and down the street.

This was ridiculous. This was one person's life. That was all.

But wasn't everyone's life important? Maybe James Price could be spoken to. Reasoned with. Maybe if the future were revealed to him he would change his ways.

Maybe.

Or maybe it would make things worse. Maybe my warning would give him even more impetus, make him more ruthless than ever. Maybe my warning was actually *part* of the future we had seen. A warning from me might show him what was possible, spurring him on to become that future monster.

There was really only one way to make certain that future did not happen.

James Price had to die.

A car meandered up the street. I was about a dozen houses away from James Price's residence as it slowed and turned into his driveway. By the time he climbed from the vehicle I was waiting across the road.

There was no mistaking him. He was James Price, the same man who had visited us in the cells, albeit forty years younger. He looked remarkably ordinary. Nothing like the monster who had threatened to lock us away for life. He grabbed some groceries from the back seat of his car before disappearing into the house.

The house sat silently in the street.

I leapt up into the air, climbing about a hundred feet. My heart was thudding inside my chest. There was another reason for killing James Price. A future with him in it would drive Brodie and Chad closer together.

Lifting my hands towards the sky, the clouds

parted and I gathered the wind to me. Since awaking with my powers, the wind had been my friend. Now that I had lost Brodie and the others, it was my only friend.

I built it into a massive sledgehammer of force, a battering ram of kinetic energy that longed to be released.

I tried to think of James Price, but all I could think of was Brodie and Chad and everything they were and everything they would become. Screaming, I brought the wind down like a mighty hammer, leveling the house to the ground.

Chapter Forty-Two

I flew without seeing.

After reducing the house to scrap, I remained above it, peering at the destruction I had created. Nothing moved in the rubble. Nothing lived. A fire started and began to consume the remains like an angry predator. The police and the fire brigade arrived. An officer produced a gun, shouted something at me and started shooting.

I soared away, not caring if I lived or died.

I had killed a man. I had taken a human life. I had committed the crime of premeditated murder. I had crossed a line that could never be uncrossed.

The wind pulled against my face and I flew on until I sighted open parkland. I fell into a quiet corner of the field and lay peering at the sky. I had killed James Price, but I had also killed myself. In delivering justice to him, I had condemned myself to a lifetime of punishment. I had lost my girlfriend, driven my friends away and now I had committed murder.

I wept.

When I next looked up, I saw the *Liber8tor* coming in to land. My dulled mind could not work out how they had found me. The hatch opened and Ebony stepped out. She ran over, dragging me to my feet. Shouting came from behind. Shots rang out. She pulled me inside *Liber8tor*.

I was dead. All I needed now was to be buried.

At some point in this unrelenting nightmare, I passed out. Awaking, I found myself slumped in a seat in the galley. Ebony and Dan were sitting at the table talking. They stopped when they saw my open eyes.

'You're onboard *Liber8tor*,' Ebony said.

I nodded.

'Do you remember what happened?' Dan asked. 'Do you remember...what you did?'

I started weeping.

'Axel.' Ferdy's voice rang out from the intercom. 'There are always possibilities. There is always hope.'

'There's no hope for me,' I said. 'I might have saved billions of lives, but I murdered someone in cold blood to do it.' A sudden thought occurred to me. 'Where are we? Are you taking me to the police?'

'No,' Ebony said, gently. 'We have a mystery on our hands and we're going off to solve it.'

'What do you mean?'

'An encrypted message was sent when the time machine first appeared over the island,' Ferdy explained. 'Ferdy was unable to break the code.'

I tried to make sense of all this. Ferdy had one of the most incredible brains on the planet, maybe *the* most incredible. 'It must have been a difficult code,' I said.

'It is almost impossible to create a code that Ferdy cannot break.'

'So how did you do it?'

'Axel was able to supply information to Ferdy that provided the key.'

This was making less sense with every passing second. I wanted to go back to sleep.

'I provided the key?' I said. 'What did I do?'

'Ferdy had already applied several billion possible keys to the code without success,' he said. 'Finally Ferdy applied a triple stacked cipher, using James Price's home address as the key.'

'And he solved it,' Dan said. 'But there's more.'

'The code was extremely complex,' Ferdy said. 'Only someone more intelligent than Ferdy would have been able to create it.'

I glanced from Ebony to Dan. 'So who made the code?'

'Ferdy,' Ferdy said.

'Ferdy?' I repeated. 'How—'

'Ferdy's future self made the code,' Ferdy explained. 'He sent it to the past so that we could solve it.'

'Why?' I asked. 'What did the message say?'

'That's the mystery,' Ebony said. 'You should come to the bridge.'

'Okay.'

Dan gripped my arm. 'Chad and Brodie are

there,' he said. 'They're not looking for any trouble.'

Neither was I. The anger was gone. I still felt a powerful sense of betrayal, but I was finished with fighting—for now. On the bridge, we found Brodie and Chad at their consoles. As they gave me a nod, I noticed Chad had a blackened eye and a bruised chin. Despite everything, I felt good about it.

Brodie continued. 'The message gave us the location of an old coal mine in Kentucky,' she said. 'We're almost there now.'

I didn't see how this would affect anything. James Price was dead and nothing was going to make him un-dead. 'We're not being pursued?'

'We had some Agency forces following, but we lost them a few hours back,' Chad said.

'We are now at the location,' Ferdy announced. 'Mine seventy-seven is directly below us.'

'Mine seventy-seven?' I said.

'That's where the message directed us,' Ebony said.

Dan took over the helm and landed the ship.

We were high in the mountains. The air was fresh and clean. The events of the last few days seemed like a bad memory. Except I couldn't rid myself of the image of James Price's home. The pile of rubble burning beneath me kept appearing in my mind's eye.

'There it is,' Brodie pointed.

The entrance to the old mine shaft was hidden behind a wall of kudzu, an invasive weed. Pulling the growth away revealed old boards and warning signs. They looked ancient. I doubted anyone had been here in years.

'We're in the middle of nowhere,' Chad said. 'Why would a future version of Ferdy send us here?'

No-one had any idea. Brodie reached up and removed some boards. Within seconds, she had created a gap large enough to climb through. Chad went first and created illumination for us. The rest of us followed close behind.

The mine had a stale, wet smell to it. Footprints were in the dirt, but faded almost beyond recognition. It was probably decades old from when the mine was abandoned. I eyed the ceiling. The supports looked ready to collapse at any moment.

We continued for another fifty feet before the glimmer of something bright stood out in the darkness. We stopped in amazement. This made no sense at all. A time machine shouldn't be sitting in this disused mine tunnel.

And yet here it was.

Chapter Forty-Three

'Why is this here?' Dan asked.

Only one person could have sent a time machine to this location.

'Ferdy,' Brodie said. 'This was Ferdy's doing.'

'This must be another test machines from an early experiment,' Ebony said.

My gut told me she was right. 'But why?' I asked. 'Why send us another time machine?'

'Ferdy must have foreseen these events,' Chad said. 'Our trip to the future. Then our return to the past.'

Brodie said to me, 'And you killing James Price.'

The machine was obviously another early model, but smaller than the others. It had no wings so it seemed unlikely it could be used for flight. It looked more like an old diving bell.

Opening the door, I peered inside. A dim light illuminated the interior. Within lay the control panel, a single seat—and something more than disturbing.

A small pile of bones. By the look of them, a human foot.

'Old Axel said some of these ships left quite unexpectedly,' Brodie grimaced.

'That's unexpected, all right,' I said, peering about the interior. 'Obviously Ferdy was determined to send it to us. Why?'

'Maybe that's why,' Ebony said, pointing at a bag. 'Aren't they temporal resonators?'

They were. In fact, there was a tool kit and a cup of dried coffee as well as the bag. A workman had been doing some work; the control panel was ajar as if it had not been screwed back into place properly. The bag contained two temporal resonators. Future Ferdy sent the time ship on its way to a time and place where it would not be found by anyone—except us.

'So the idea is for us to use the time machine,' I said slowly.

'And we can come back,' Chad said. 'There's another temporal resonator to bring us home.'

It all seemed very strange, but then I knew there could only be one reason for this. 'Ferdy wanted us to see the future,' I said. 'Now that I've changed history, he wanted us to see the results.'

'That makes sense,' Ebony said.

So I climbed into the seat and warmed up the machine. This was definitely an earlier model. I set the time machine for the current date forty years in the future. We slammed the hatch shut, remembering too late that we had not discarded the human bones. Everyone tried not to look at them. I started the machine, the ship shuddered and the familiar black pools flowed past.

A shape appeared. It wasn't the familiar blue strip of sky we had seen before. Instead it was just another circle of blackness. It grew larger and larger. The time machine lurched again and shook badly for another minute before it finally grew still.

We had arrived.

'We're there,' Brodie said.

'Or here,' Ebony said. 'Depending on how you look at it.'

Chad eased the door open. Ice broke off the hull as we stepped out. We were still in the mine tunnel. The time machine had moved in time, but not space. Chad created a fire, illuminating the tunnel.

It had felt cold before, but now it was hot. Very hot. I broke into a sweat.

Brodie wiped her face. 'Why is it so humid?'

'I don't know,' I said.

Dan pointed down at the floor. 'There's our footprints.'

He was correct. They were our footprints, but the ground had been wet underfoot when we entered the tunnel. Now it was hard and dry. We made our way up the tunnel and found that someone had long since repaired the boards. A strange crimson light leaked through the cracks between the timbers.

Brodie punched hard at a couple of pieces and we climbed through. It was hot in the tunnel, but even hotter outside. I expected it to be midday. Instead I saw the sun was low in a dull auburn-colored sky. It had just risen.

'Oh my God,' Ebony said. 'What happened?'

Smoke was everywhere. A fire had ripped through here, reducing the forest to gray cinders. It reminded me of the surface of the moon. Breathing was difficult; the air was choked with the smell of burnt plastic.

Liber8tor was gone, obviously retrieved by the Agency at some time in the past. They had not thought to search the mine shaft or we would have seen their footprints.

'I'm going up to take a look,' I said.

'Be careful,' Brodie said.

I didn't answer. Leaping into the air, I flew over the landscape. The air was different to anything I'd ever experienced. It was thicker, almost soup-like in its consistency. The terrain appeared the same in every direction, as if devastated by some terrible disaster, a wave of destruction that had burned everything in its path.

Lexington was one of the largest cities in Kentucky. I flew towards it cautiously. The skies in James Price's world were zealously guarded by the Agency. They might be guarded here too. But the further I flew, the more I saw how completely different this world was. No birds soared through the air. Nothing lived on the ground. No plant life. No animals. No people. It was as if everything had been decimated in one terrible moment.

Reaching the city, I slowly descended to a narrow street. All the buildings were burnt here too as if a fire had raced through. The sun was now a little higher in the sky, but the illumination stayed the same, everything lit by an eerie red glow.

I found a news agency—or what remained of it. The glass door had shattered years before. I stepped through to find most of the interior burnt out. A skeleton lay behind the counter, a melted food container next to it. Whatever had happened here had been sudden; the owner had not had time to flee.

Most of the magazines had been reduced to ashes, but a few piles of newspapers were relatively intact. I pulled away the top charred copies, revealing a headline.

Agency Promises Swift Retaliation with

Superweapon

My hands shook as I read the article. It said the Agency government had decided to continue its expansion in response to the 'terrorist' activities of the United Nations. Pulling apart another pile of papers, I uncovered a headline that turned my blood cold.

It's War

A coalition of nations had decided to retaliate against the Agency. Some analysts warned about the use of a new 'scorched Earth' weapon currently in development by the Agency. They were concerned it could result in the destruction of all life on the planet.

Dropping the newspapers, I stumbled to the street. How was this possible? I had killed James Price. It should have made the world a better place. Instead, the time line had taken a terrible step in the wrong direction, the end result being global annihilation.

What had gone wrong?

Rounding a corner, I found myself facing a huge billboard. Burnt by the scorching of the planet, enough had survived to make it recognizable. I had already seen the caption before.

The Agency is your friend

Last time I had seen it, the poster had been emblazoned with the image of the Agency's leader, James Price. Now I stared at it in disbelief.

'No,' I moaned. 'It's not possible.'

Falling to my knees in horror, I recognized the Agency's leader all too well.

Gazing back at me was my own face.

Chapter Forty-Four

How was it possible? How could I have become the leader of the Agency? How could I have been so filled with hatred that I would try to dominate the planet—and then be prepared to destroy it?

But deep in my heart I already knew the answer.

It all had to do with Brodie and Chad, and my sense of betrayal. From that had risen a hatred, not just for them, but for everything the world had to offer. My hatred had destroyed me and the planet.

Had Old Axel been aware of all this? Maybe. He wouldn't have foreseen the end of the world, but he probably knew I would want revenge on those who had let me down.

My eyes fell to a shape in a nearby doorway. I stumbled over, tenderly picking it up. It was a doll, its face blackened by the blast, its clothing burnt away. I tried to imagine the owner of it, a girl who had loved and cherished it. Her parents must have been worried in those days leading up to the end, but they must have taken solace in the hope that reason would prevail.

They won't use the weapon, they must have told each other. *No-one would be that insane.*

I took to the skies again and returned to the mine where I told the others everything I had seen, finishing with the billboard with my face on it.

Most of them looked shocked, but Brodie's face crumpled into tears. She angrily wiped them away, realizing, I think, that our relationship lay at the heart of this terrible disaster.

'So the world is doomed,' Dan said. 'It's going to be destroyed in some terrible war.'

'We have to stop it,' Ebony said. 'If we can.'

'We might be able to,' Brodie said, angrily wiping away her tears. 'We know that by changing the past again, we can change the future.'

Was that possible? Could it be that easy?

'Maybe,' Ebony said. 'But how do we know that this future doesn't stem from this journey?'

'What are you saying?' I asked her.

'Maybe it's not as easy as going back and

making different decisions. Maybe all those decisions, including our decision to visit the future, led to this.'

'The other future was bad enough,' Brodie said. 'This one's even worse.'

'So you're saying none of this would have happened if I hadn't killed James Price?'

'Both futures are a disaster. There's got to be something better than either of them.'

I felt miserable. 'There must have been another way of stopping James Price,' I said. 'I wish I hadn't killed him.'

'Undoing that would be a good start,' Dan said.

Ebony's head jerked up. 'That's it.'

'What?' I asked.

'We can change things! We have a time machine!' she said. 'We can go back and stop all this from happening.'

'But what do we change?' I asked.

'What do you think?'

I swallowed. 'But I've already killed James

Price...'

Brodie frowned. 'Maybe you can stop yourself from killing him,' she said.

'You know what Ferdy would say,' Dan said. 'It would be a gross violation of the space/time continuum—'

'Sounds serious,' Chad said.

'—and the annihilation of all matter in every multi-verse.'

'Okay, it sounds *really* serious.'

Ebony spoke up. 'Did you actually see James Price die?'

'No. But he was inside the building.'

'Are you sure?'

The seed of an idea began to grow in my mind. 'I didn't see him die,' I said. 'I might be able to save him if I can get back before I destroy the house.'

Dan frowned. 'But you can't let you...er...your past self see your current self.'

'I know,' I said. 'It would be a violation...multi-verse...thing...'

We hurried to the time machine. Climbing

aboard, I adjusted the dial for five hours prior to our original departure. 'That should give me enough time to get to James Price's house and save him.'

I activated the machine. Once again it shuddered badly in flight as it returned to the past. We tumbled out of the craft. We had used up the temporal resonators sent with the time ship to the past. There would be no other opportunities to change history. It was this or nothing.

We ran from the cave into the light of a new day. The others started towards *Liber8tor*.

'I think you guys should lay low,' I said.

'But we can help you,' Brodie protested.

'There's already enough versions of ourselves running around. We can't risk you running into yourselves. I'll see you back here in twelve hours,' I said, trying to smile. 'Go and drink hot chocolates.'

I leapt up into the sky. Dawn broke, casting yellow fingers of light across the landscape. It was a beautiful day on a beautiful world. Who in their right mind would want to destroy it?

Arriving in New York with an hour to spare, I

made my way to James Price's address. Careful to stay out of sight, I hid under a tree in the backyard where I could watch the driveway. Only a few minutes passed before I saw someone I recognized all too well walking down the street, their eyes fixed on the house.

Me.

It was strange, like watching a distorted version of myself in a mirror. I looked so suspicious, so *angry*, I was amazed a neighbor hadn't rung the police. A chill danced up and down my spine. I recognized something else too. The same bitter expression that Old Axel had always worn.

Finally I heard a car pull into the driveway. James Price climbed out and went inside. Creeping to the back door, I used my powers to force the lock. By the time I found James Price, he was already putting his groceries away into the refrigerator.

His mouth fell open in amazement. 'Who the hell are you?' he asked. 'What are you doing in my house?'

I glanced out the window where a storm was

starting to build.

'Saving your life,' I said, forming a barrier around us.

Chapter Forty-Five

We sat in *Liber8tor*'s galley eating in silence. We were all there; Brodie, Chad, Dan, Ebony and—of course—the ever present Ferdy. We had been back on the island for three days taking such much needed R&R. There had been no sign of my future self; he had not returned. Whatever we had done in the present had changed the future. How much it had changed was impossible to say.

James Price had been grateful I saved his life. In return, I asked him a favor. 'Please try to do good,' I said. 'For everyone's sake.'

He promised he would, but there was a problem with that. Everyone's definition of good is different. Through some misguided sense of right, he might still become the head of the Agency. He might still become a dictator. He might still destroy the planet with his experiments.

Only time would tell.

Ferdy broke the silence. 'Ferdy believes he has an explanation for the boy that Dan met,' he said.

'Would you like to hear it?'

'Sure,' I said.

Anything to break the silence.

'It would seem that Doctor Satou was partially successful in his attempts to create a hybrid plant/animal,' Ferdy continued. 'His final work would seem to have been a combining of human cells with mold.'

'That's...revolting,' Ebony said.

'So Henry was...mold?' Brodie asked.

'Mold spores,' Ferdy said. 'And so was the creature.'

'How is that possible?'

'Mold is microscopic. It would seem the spores were able to combine and manipulate its appearance into either the character of Doctor Jekyll or Mr. Hyde.'

'But why was he a boy?' Dan asked. 'And whose skeleton was in the cell?'

'The skeleton would appear to have been a US navy seaman who was captured during the war. We'll never know his identity, but his one personal possession was the copy of Robert Louis Stevenson's *Dr Jekyll and Mr Hyde*. The man was infected by Doctor Satou's spores and eventually died.'

'And he became...' Ebony's voice trailed away.

'Something new,' Ferdy said. 'A new form of life with no identity of its own.'

'So it took the identities of Doctor Jekyll and Mr. Hyde?' Chad asked. 'But Doctor Jekyll isn't a child in the book.'

'We'll never know why Henry took the form of a child. Maybe he was responding to Dan or possibly the seaman's last memories were of his childhood. That will forever remain a mystery.'

Everyone finished eating and went away to do other things, leaving Brodie and me alone in the galley.

'I can understand if you want to be with Chad,' I said.

'I don't want to be with Chad!' she said, rolling her eyes. 'Chad's just a friend. He'll never be anything else.'

'Never?'

That made her pause. We had both discovered that nobody—with the possible exception of Ferdy—knew the future.

'I'm not interested in being with him,' she said, firmly. 'I'm not even sure I want to be with you.'

I nodded. My heart was breaking, but I understood what she was saying. We'd been through a crazy couple of months. Our memories were taken, we were given super powers and then Brodie and I involved in the greatest love story since *Gone with the Wind*. It was a lot for anyone.

'Is it Dan?' I asked. 'Do you want to be with Dan?'

Brodie burst out laughing, rolling her eyes. 'I don't want to be with anyone!' she said. 'I'm not an accessory. I can exist without being attached to a guy!'

The intercom buzzed. 'This is Ferdy,' he said. 'There are Agency ships heading in our direction. They appear to be on an intercept course.'

Damn. That was the end of our island hideaway.

We assembled on the bridge. Dan took his place at the helm while the others checked their consoles. Ebony suggested possible escape routes as Chad brought up the weapon systems. He glanced at me. I nodded and he returned the gesture. Our bruises were fading, but some wounds would take longer to heal. I still felt a deep hurt, but I had seen the path of hatred. I knew where it could lead and I wouldn't let it control my life.

Liber8tor soared into the sky.

None of us knew what the future held. Our friendship had taken a battering, but it wasn't too late to mend fences.

There was still time.

A Few Final Words

I hope you enjoyed reading The Twisted Future. The other books in the Teen Superheroes series are:

Diary of a Teenage Superhero (Book One)

The Doomsday Device (Book Two)

The Battle for Earth (Book Three)

Terminal Fear (Book Five)

Thanks again and happy reading!

Darrell